The Impulsive Imp

HOWARD O'BRIEN

THE IMPULSIVE IMP

2007

The Impulsive Imp

For K

PREFACE

Howard O'Brien wrote *The Impulsive Imp* in the late 1940s to entertain his eldest daughters, Alice and Anne, who later achieved recognition as the novelists Alice Borchardt and Anne Rice. Our family preserved the novel unpublished. I retyped it in 1976 because Howard's manuscript was fading to illegibility. I retyped it again in 2002, working from a photocopy of Howard's manuscript, in order to put it on a digital platform.

This edition is entirely the work of Howard O'Brien with slight copyediting and two minor content changes made on behalf of young readers. To be specific, I corrected occasional typing errors, normalized capitalization and punctuation, and modernized the spelling of compound words that are no longer hyphenated. With regard to content, I repositioned the razor blade that the Imp discovers in the middle of the bathroom floor to a spot behind the clothes hamper where it might plausibly lie unnoticed. I also removed a pack of cigarettes from the list of items that the Father puts in his pockets before leaving for work because it is now generally considered bad form to portray role models in children's fiction as smokers.

Howard understandably made Roddy, the singing mouse, a member of a fictitious genus species. However, Roddy's narrative about the zoology of rats is genuinely scientific. Howard composed *The Impulsive Imp* shortly after returning to his New Orleans home from the Veterans Hospital at Mare Island, California, where he cared for patients during World War II. The novel's allusions to transcontinental travel and trauma medicine appear to have been inspired by its author's wartime service.

Tamara Tinker
2009

CHAPTER 1

The house was old. It looked tired like an old man's face. It had been painted, repainted and painted again; and there were cracks in the paint like wrinkles on an old man's cheek. At night, however, its windows glowed like young eyes under an old man's untidy brows.

Inside there was a grate with a wide stone hearth. Running up through the roof was a spacious brick chimney down which Santa Claus, were he twice as stout, could slide without scratching his buckle.

In the fireplace, this night, logs were burning. On a thick rug in front of the grate sat a girl and a boy. He was named Alan and she, Alice; and they sat quiet. It was not often they were quiet. Usually they had a thousand questions to ask and as many things to do; therefore their father was astonished to see them so quiet.

"What marvel has come to pass," he said to them, "that my magpies have become owls?"

Alan looked up. He was seven and the older. He frowned a shade of a frown. "You say things sometimes, Daddy, and I don't know what you mean."

"Most of the time," explained the father, "you and Alice jabber like magpies, but tonight you are silent as owls."

"Why are owls silent?" asked Alice. Naturally she did not know why owls are silent, because she was only five years old.

"Well," said the father, "most people think owls are silent because they are wise. But the fact is that owls are silent because they're stupid."

"How do you know they're stupid?" Alan wanted to know.

"Because they stay awake all night," exclaimed the father. "You and Alice don't want to be stupid, so get you off to bed."

"The night has too much hours," complained Alice. "Me and Alan will sit and watch the logs burning—and that's for today." She dipped her head emphatically in the fashion of her mother.

"You'll get off to bed before a lamb can shake half his tail," stated the father. "And that's for sure."

"You're a mean Daddy if you make us go to bed," Alice declared. "The fire is fuller of pictures than television."

"It seems to me," the father said, "that you might be a mean girl if you don't do what I say."

"I'm Alice, and I'm a good girl!"

"To be sure you are," the father soothed her. "Now look at one last picture to think about in bed."

"I'm looking hard," said Alan, and he screwed up his eyes and his mouth screwed up also.

"I'm looking big," Alice said, and she opened her eyes wide like saucers. The flames danced in her eyes as in a mirror, and made the tendrils of her hair traceries of gold.

"What do you see?" the father inquired.

"I see a white horse." Alan breathed hard. "He has a long red tail, and he's blowing fire through his nose."

"I see Cinderella," Alice smiled, "and she has on the goldenest slippers."

"Glass slippers." The father corrected.

"No, gold slippers," insisted Alice. "This a different Cinderella, and I'm her fairy grandmother."

"And so to bed." The father gathered them up. They bathed their faces and hands. The mother came and said night prayers with them, and tucked them under the blankets.

"Daddy, O Daddy!" Alan called.

"Yes?" The father stood in the doorway.

"I'm going to be a good boy in school tomorrow."

"You're always a good boy," the father assured him. "Some days you're gooder than other days."

"You mean 'better,' Daddy."

The father laughed. "Maybe it's a good school after all."

"Daddy, O a-Daddy!" Alice called.

The father went into her bedroom. "You stayed too long with Alan," she chided, "I'm too sleepy now to give you all my kisses."

"I'm most honored to have even one," the father bowed.

"I'll give you my velvet." She touched her father's cheek with her lips.

"It was so soft," her father said, "just like velvet."

"You missed the Princess kiss and the Strawberry ice-cream kiss."

"Is it possible for one man to have missed so much?"

"Tomorrow night you'll come sooner?"

"Horses couldn't hold me away," the father promised.

"Do horses really blow fire from their noses?"

"Only in make believe," the father told her.

"Please don't tell Alan. 'Cus he thinks he's going to have a horse someday that blows fire all the time out of its nose."

"He'll be satisfied with an ordinary horse. Now, good-night, dear."

"Daddy?"

"No more questions tonight."

"Just one more," Alice pleaded. "A little question."

"All right," the father granted. "A little one."

"Was Cinderella really in the grate?"

The father rubbed his nose with the back of his finger. "No, I don't think she was, but it's not important so long as she was in your mind."

"What's 'important' mean?"

"'Important' means you had better go to sleep right away."

"I been going to sleep all the time," Alice sighed. "I don't know if I'm asleep or awake, and it feels so good. Like everything is warm and nice."

The father tightened the tuck of the blanket, and Alice half opened one eye. "Will you put my dolls in front of the grate so they won't be cold?"

The father promised he would while his kiss slid off her cheek as she burrowed her face into the crook of her arm.

Having put the two dolls, Dan and Mary Jane, close enough to the grate to be warm but not so close as to catch fire, the father sank down into his chair. He stared at the burning logs, and tried to see Cinderella. His eyes began to water, but Cinderella did not come. Then he tried to see a white horse blowing fire and smoke from its nostrils. There was no horse, only white and red flames that licked along the logs like dogs' tongues.

The mother came in and leaned over his shoulder. "Why so pensive?" she asked. He wrinkled his forehead as he refocused his eyes, and said rather sadly: "I can't see Cinderella in the grate, nor can I see a white horse—or any kind of horse for that matter. But especially I can't see a white horse blowing fire and smoke from its nose."

"You should go to bed," she advised him.

"Can you see Cinderella?"

"I can see gingham," she replied lightly, "and the pedal of my sewing machine flying up and down."

"That's better, I guess," admitted the father, "but tonight I'd rather see Cinderella." With a grunt he pushed himself up from the chair, and, taking the poker, prodded the logs. A shower of sparks flew up the chimney as the logs broke. He shoved the burning fragments as far back as he could, and he and the mother went off to bed.

High in the chimney there was a hole left by a brick that had fallen out long ago. No doubt it had broken into bits on the hearthstone, and the bits had been swept up, thrown away and forgotten. No one knew of the hole. Had anyone known, he would have given it no second thought; for it was no serious matter. But the vacancy high in the darkness was a lonesome, hidden place that had become half filled with soot. Embedded in the soot and grit was a splinter of oak. The splinter was dried and blackened from the heat of many fires; but once it had lived within the white heart of a splendid tree.

The oak tree had stood proud on a wide plantation near the city of New Orleans. Gracing the earth it had proffered its beauty of symmetry and the cool of its shade for the pleasure and comfort of men. But men, with a perverted sense of honor, used its shade but for a shelter from the sun while they fought, dueling, seeking one another's blood.

One day a young man fell, a rapier's thrust having reached his heart. Before the blood stained the fine cambric of his shirt, he was dead. He was the plantation owner's son; and, in the shade of the oak where he had played as a child, he died even before he was a man. And the planter, in anguish with the knowledge that his son's life of promise had been ended by folly, ordered his slaves to fell the tree. In the spread of its shade more than twenty men had died for trifles.

The fiber of the oak protested the axe's edge. The breeze in the gnarled branches whispered the innocence of the tree;

but the planter, weeping, commanded the slaves to work in shifts that there would be no pause in the sweep of the axes. Finally, its trunk cut almost through, the tree crashed down, its branches cracking off with noise like pistol fire. The stronger branches, however, held up the crown; and it lay like a warrior, fallen mortally wounded, braced up by arms from ultimate collapse. The planter cursed the tree he had loved, but under which had died his son whom he had loved infinitely more.

From this cursed oak, long since gone into the rot of the ground, had been preserved the splinter lodged in the chimney of the house where Alan and Alice lay sleeping, undreaming. When the logs were struck with the poker and the swarm of sparks sped up the chimney, this enchanted splinter was set afire. The little cave was lighted up momentarily while the splinter crackled in blaze. There remained but a small amount of pungent smoke that dribbled away. And when it was gone, the cave had an occupant. Yes, there was someone or something there.

A little creature stirred, stretching. Some of the soot was shoved from the cave and fell down into the grate like a light sprinkle of rain. There was a small sneeze like a cat sneezing, and more grit sprinkled down into the grate. Then there was a scratching sound of fingernails on brick. The creature that had been born in the little cave high in the chimney was coming down. He gripped the creases between the bricks and came down quickly. Into the grate from the chimney came a tail in half a curl. It was so dark a green it was almost black. On its end was a barb, two-pointed like the tip of an old Indian arrow. As the tail descended, a flame from the burning logs licked at it. With a squeal of surprise the creature scrambled up the chimney back to the cave. It was an imp, no doubt about it. What else would have a tail twice as long as its body, and, on the tip of the tail, a barb? He was an impulsive imp to have come scratching down the chimney as soon as he was born.

The father was pulling on his pajamas when he heard the squeal. The mother asked him, "Did you hear that? Was it Alice or Alan?"

"One of them must be having a dream," he replied. He listened but heard nothing more. "Everything is all right," he assured the mother, "Let's go to sleep. For Alice the night has 'too much' hours; for me the night doesn't have nearly enough. There ought to be two nights for every one day."

CHAPTER 2

The Impulsive Imp sat in his cave. He put the tip of his tail to his mouth and licked the spot that was scorched. He trembled with anger. Less than five minutes old and his whole body was shaking with anger. It was unfortunate that his first real emotion should be anger and even more than anger. In truth, he was in a rage. His ears were shaped like the spatulate end of a tablespoon, and, in his rage, they shook like leaves growing close to a branch. His nose was like a doorknob and it seemed to palpitate with his wrath. His mouth had the sweet shape of a heart while his chin was the point of a larger heart, but his mouth was all twisted out of shape with anger, and his chin trembled so that he almost bit his tongue as he licked the blister at the tip of his tail. His eyes were like the end of a "Lucifer" match: pupils of white like the phosphorous and ringed around with red like the sulfur. They appeared ready to burst into flame at any moment.

As soon as the throb in his tail died down to a small echo of pain, he wrapped his tail twice around his body and began to sweep out his cave. He crawled on hands and knees, shoving the soot toward the edge. When he had accumulated a heap at the brink, he gave a hearty shove, and the soot and grit showered down upon the glowing logs. Looking down the chimney the Impulsive Imp saw that the logs were only embers that glowed like big fiery eyes. He was still angry over the blister on his tail, and he took personal affront from the eyes of the embers looking up into his own. He impolitely spat at the embers. He was such a small imp with such a small capacity for spitting that his spittle failed to make a sizzle loud enough for him to hear. His sizzle was a fizzle, and did not calm his anger in the least. He frowned, and his frown was like a wrinkled piece of thread across his forehead. He growled as loudly as he could, but his growling was no louder than that you hear coming from your own stomach. Holding the top edge of the cave, he leaned out to his full height, and he was as high as a new pencil standing on its point.

"I'm going to take me an imp down there," he snarled, "and be spitting all over them embers."

Keeping his tail coiled close around his waist, he climbed down the chimney again. At the bottom he hugged the side of the grate and stepped with care. The ashes were warm around his feet and between his toes. Safely he reached the outer edge of the hearth stone and leaped out onto the rug where Alan and Alice had sat not long before. In the grate a few embers still glowed. He ran to the edge of the rug and stepped to the floor. He would throw the rug upon the embers and extinguish them. His tugging was in vain, for he was too small an imp for so large a rug. He gnashed his teeth, and the sound was like that you make when walking on the sugar that always spills when the sugar bowl is filled. The Imp liked the sound. He gnashed again and said:

"I am being most ferocious!"

He was so taken up with the noise of his gnashing that he dropped the end of the rug. Putting hands on hips he gnashed the teeth on the right side of his mouth, then the teeth on the left. He gritted the teeth in front. Finally he gnashed all his teeth together in a storm of gnashing. He boasted aloud: "No doubting I am the most ferocious imp in the whole world!"

Suddenly, like stars going out in the morning, the embers lost their light and were only dead gray ashes. For a moment there was a memory of warmth; then they were cold. In the grate remained only the ghost of the fire that had flamed so warmly, containing a prancing white horse and a lovely Cinderella. In a dark room even embers make a great light, and when they died out the Imp felt lonely. He was a little imp in a big room in a strange house.

"The trouble with being born from an enchanted splinter," he sighed, "is that I am having no mamma and no papa, no sisters and no brothers, and I am plumb naked to booting."

He looked around the room. Because he was an imp he could see in the dark. He saw the legs of the chairs going up from the floor like tall pine trees. Since there were rungs running from leg to leg he knew he could climb the chairs. He would have been interested had he not been lonely. He went to one chair and pushed with all his might. It rocked back and forth enticing him to ride, but he was too lonely. He gnashed his teeth furiously to raise his spirits, but it helped not a jot. He saw the bookcase, and, taking a spread-leg stance before, read the titles.

"I'll be reading one of these books someday," he promised himself, "and I will be the smartest imp in the whole world. Not tonight, though, 'cus right now I'm too busy being the loneliest imp in the whole world."

Added to lonesomeness was hunger. The Imp's stomach was empty as two mirrors facing each other. Being newborn, he was not sure just what he could eat.

"Maybe, if I am eating one of these pretty books it will be friendly in my stomach," he mused. "I'm seeming to remember that someone said a good book should be digested."

He uncoiled his tail from around his waist and tossed it so the barb hooked on to the second shelf of the bookcase. Climbing up the tail he reached the shelf and perched. One of the books, bound in green leather, was entitled *Huckleberry Finn*.

"This, no doubting, will be the berries," he declared, and began chewing vigorously at page nine. "This is tasting hardly better than soot and cinders," he paused to complain, and then took another bite to see if the taste would improve. It did not. He belched suddenly and fell from the shelf. Luckily the barb was still caught on the shelf, and his tail held him up just short of the floor where he swung back and forth like a pendulum.

"Something is being bad in that book," he snorted, "either the huckleberries or the Finns."

He climbed up again and turned back to the first page of the book. "No wonder it is being bad," he stated. "Published in 1908. The whole thing is being stale."

He walked along the shelf looking for another book that might be more appetizing. Finding one entitled *Strange Fruit*, and thinking it might be fresher since it was published in 1945, he bit heartily into page four. Immediately he spat and sucked in his cheeks.

"This is being rotten like nothing is rotting before!" he exclaimed. "I will be staying away from strange fruits for all time."

Deciding to look elsewhere for something to eat the Imp slid down from the shelf and started out across the room. In passing, he chinned himself three times on the rung of the rocking chair and found he was being mighty weak for lack of food.

"O mying," he sighed, "my stomach is empty as a candy-box in kindergarten."

Leaving the living room the Imp entered a long hall that ran the length of the house. At the other end was an alcove. On one side of the alcove was an arched entrance to the kitchen of the house, and on the other side was a similar entrance to a bedroom where slept the mother and the father. Against the further wall of the alcove stood an antique hat rack and cabinet combined. It was decorated with much gingerbread work and miniature balconies supported by little posts resting on the backs of diminutive mahogany figures. Set in the hat rack, a little off center to the right, was a mirror extending from the bottom almost to the top. The mirror was wonderfully clear, and moonlight flooding in through the kitchen window fell upon it.

When the Imp looked down the hall, he saw himself reflected. He did not know it was his own image in the mirror, and his eyes popped out at the sight. He leaped a full two inches into the air, snatched his tail and dashed for the chimney. About to clamber up, he made pause to ponder: "That other one is not being so large." He cocked his ears and heard nothing pursuing him.

"I'm a ferocious imp," he encouraged himself, "and I can lick anything my size even if it's an elephant."

Having crept back, he looked down the hall again.

"Ho, ho, it is still being there," he said. Peering intently he discovered that the other had a long tail also barbed. "It is being another imp," and he laughed for joy. "I will bandy words with him."

He shouted: "Hello!" His voice was as loud as the ticking of a grandfather clock. The imp in the mirror made no answer.

"Hello! Hello!" the Impulsive Imp cried impatiently. "He is being an enemy," he decided when he failed to get a response. He clenched his fists and cocked them bellicosely. The imp in the mirror did the same. The Impulsive Imp executed a fast jig to exhibit his footwork; and the imp in the alcove jigged as well.

"This will be the handsomest fight," cried the Impulsive Imp as he started on the run down the long hall. Naturally, the imp in the mirror ran also. "I will run faster than him," growled the Impulsive Imp, "to show that I'm not being afraid." He flew down the hall. Suddenly there rang out a bong as though a dinner gong had been struck with a padded mallet. "I am being hit with a foul," groaned the Imp as he sat plump upon the floor. He rubbed his head with the palm of his hand while studying himself with wonder in the mirror.

"Why, it is being me" he muttered. "And I am being almost killed in meeting myself." Abruptly he stopped massaging his scalp for he heard the mother's voice.

"I heard a noise," the mother declared, "I'm sure I heard a noise."

"There are always noises," grumbled the father sleepily. "The world is full of noises. Even trees make a noise when they're growing."

"What I heard was not a tree growing," the mother asserted.

"Maybe a very big tree—" proffered the father.

"YOU're ridiculous," the mother told him.

"I'm just sleepy."

"Don't you think you should go see what made the noise?" the mother persisted.

"Probably it was a mouse. Just a little harmless mouse."

The Impulsive Imp pouted his lips. He was about to shout that he was not being a mouse, but he caught himself just in time. The mother spoke for him:

"It was not a mouse I heard."

"Then it must have been the floor creaking," the father pretended with finality and hugged his pillow for further sleep.

"It was not a creak," the mother informed him.

"My dear," sighed the father, "you've told me just about everything it couldn't be. Couldn't you tell me what it was, and we'll go back to sleep."

"I don't know what it was, but I think you should get up to see. It might have been a burglar."

"If I were a burglar I wouldn't make any noise. Why should a burglar go around making noise?"

"I'm going myself!" The mother was fully exasperated.

"No, don't," the father restrained her. "I'm going this very minute." He snapped on the light and fumbled under the bed for his slippers. "Investigating noises," he grumbled. "Waste of time—good sleeping time. Whatever made the noise might be four miles from here making some more noise to get some other weary husband out of bed. I don't even know where the noise was."

"It was right out in the alcove," the mother told him.

The father shuffled toward the alcove. The Imp had been so taken up by the father's nocturnal nonsense that he had given no thought to his own safety. Having suffered the pain of a blistered tail and the shock of a head-on collision with an unyielding mirror, he expected kindness from no one. He was sure that the whole world was against him and everything that stirred his enemy. When he realized the father was approaching the alcove it was too late for flight back to his cave. He sped to the left into the moonlit kitchen. His tail dragged behind him, and the blister rubbed on the kitchen floor. The first thing that caught his eye was a green plastic ring at the end of a window shade string. He leaped for the string in order to climb up and get his blister free of the floor. When his weight, slight as it was, hit the ring, the shade went racing up with an angry clatter. The Imp thought his stomach would escape through his toes. His heels flew out and his tail smacked down on the floor, and in a trice he was high in the air. So sudden was his ascent that he lost the breath he would have used to scream. The shade wound around the stick, and when it was fully wound the stick continued to turn. The Imp, like the end boy in a "crack-the-whip" game, felt a terrific jerk when the string also began to wind around. He could not hold on. He was snapped from the ring. As gracefully as a trapeze artist he somersaulted through the air, and landed with a jolt on top of the kitchen cabinet. There he lay wondering if the world had suddenly ended.

When the shade rattled around the stick the father jumped back into the bedroom.

"It's a robber with a machine gun," he cried. Pressing his hands to his stomach, he turned to the mother who was sitting up in bed. "I believe I'm riddled through the middle," he gasped.

The mother burst into laughter. "Why, it's the shade in the kitchen."

"How do you know?" he demanded, examining his hands for blood.

"It's gone up like that twice this week."

"Why doesn't somebody fix it?" he complained.

"Someone has fixed it."

"Who?"

"You!"

The father scratched his head. "I guess I'll buy a new one," he decided.

Bare feet came pattering down the hall. It was Alice in her blue sleeper. The father sank down on the bed. He closed one eye and looked wearily at Alice through the other. "It's the delegation from the third room," he announced with a sigh.

"I'm Alice," said Alice, "and there's too much noise."

"Go back to bed immediately," the father told her, "and walk on your toes, or you'll have the soles of your sleeper all dirty."

"When is the night gonna be over?" she inquired.

"Too soon," he informed her, "much too soon. Now please go back to bed."

"Will you stir me a little first," she pleaded.

"All right," he granted, "approach quickly for the stirring."

Alice rested her head on his knees while he rubbed her back with a gentle circular motion. "Now you're stirred thoroughly." He lifted her and carried her back to bed.

When the father returned to his bedroom, the mother was deep in sleep.

Kicking off his slippers, he muttered: "It's a wonderful life—if you can call it living."

CHAPTER 3

Stillness crept through the house again and settled down in all the corners. The Impulsive Imp raised his head and shook it clear. Planting his elbows on the top of the kitchen cabinet, he cupped his chin in his hands.

"No doubting," he bemoaned, "I am the most misfortunate imp in the whole world. I will be an old, worn out imp before I am having a chance to be young."

Tears gathered in his eyes and were about to wash over the sadness of his face. He began to sniffle and, in sniffling, he sniffed, and in sniffing he forgot to sniffle, because his mouth began to water.

"What is this sweet thing," he exulted, raising his head from his hands, "that is coming to my nose and making my stomach glad it is empty?"

He explored the top of the kitchen cabinet with his nose. He found nothing but dust. Hooking the barb of his tail to the top of the cabinet, he let himself down slowly, sniffing ten sniffs a second. Whatever was so good was inside the cabinet. Clutching his tail with one hand, he unlatched the cabinet door. It sprang open an inch or so, and the aroma struck his nose with such intensity that he almost lost his grip. Grasping his tail with both hands, he pushed the door wide with his feet and swung inside the cabinet. The cookie jar drew him like a magnet, drew him so forcibly that he snubbed his nose against its side. From the bottom of an overturned cup he climbed up to the rim of the cookie jar, over the mouth of which was spread a cloth. He lifted the cloth and the fragrance unhinged his thinking. His teeth began to click as he tried to chew the very spice in the air. He leaped down into the jar, a leap of no distance, for the jar was better than half-full.

In less than two ticks of a fast clock he had a cookie in his mouth. It was necessary for him to turn it like a slow disc because his mouth could fit only over the edge. He ate so fast and turned so rapidly that when the cookie was done he bit his thumb twice before he could halt his jaws. Gradually he slowed down to a steady munching, savoring the taste as though it were the ultimate ecstasy. He ate until his jaws grew tired and he could no longer hold a cookie to his mouth, until shamefully few cookies remained.

Leaning against the side of the jar, he tried to fold his hands on his stomach, but his fingers could not come together across his swollen middle. He sighed for satisfaction.

"Where there is being food I guess I am being the biggest glutton in the world."

The Imp glanced up. A cockroach looked down at him from the rim of the jar. Standing very still on the stilts of its legs, the roach fanned the air slowly with its feelers and looked accusingly at the Imp.

"You are being a little fellow who should be starting no trouble," the Imp advised the cockroach. "There is nothing here for you to be eating."

The other continued to wave its feelers deliberately.

"What is being your name?" the Imp inquired. The roach's only answer was the elliptical motion of its whiskers.

"You are acting dumb like a bell without a bonger," the Imp charged the roach. "Go wave your feathers at somebody else." He rapped his knuckles against the side of the cookie jar, and the cockroach scurried away with sounds like sand shaking in a paper bag.

"I guess he knows I am being a most ferocious imp," the Imp murmured through a yawn; and, delighting in the thought of the cookies, he fell asleep working his jaws the while like an old man who has lost all his teeth.

Suddenly there appeared over the rim of the jar the head of the cockroach that had scurried away. With it came another and another until their heads were around the mouth of the jar like beads on a necklace. Solemnly they stood and studied the Imp. Slowly and more slowly moved their feelers. Then they crossed their feelers, one over the other, until a mesh like mosquito netting covered the mouth of the jar. Of a sudden in a grating chorus they screamed at the Impulsive Imp:

"You ate all the cookies! We'll not let you out. We'll never let you out! You ate all the cookies!"

The Imp sprang up out of sleep. He plopped down again under the weight of his distended stomach. Fearfully he looked up. Not a single cockroach was on the rim of the jar. No feelers; no scream over the jar's mouth. He rubbed his eyes to make sure that sleep was gone.

"A most frightening dream to be having," gasped the Imp. "I will be hating cockroaches forever. Everybody is being enemies—even in my dreamings."

He struggled to his feet, and his stomach pulled him forward causing him to stoop like a dwarf with a humpback. When he raised his hands he could not reach the opening of the jar.

"This is most embarrassment." He giggled a little at his plight to lessen its gravity. He looped his tail and threw it so that the barb would catch on the edge of the jar. Because his stomach was an obstruction he could use only one hand. Twice he failed to throw the tail high enough. It snaked down, the barb rapping him on the head.

"Ei, yi!" he cried, "I am beating myself to death with my own tail."

Mustering his full strength the Imp hurled the tail a third time. It sailed through the mouth of the jar, and the barb caught fast to the rim. He began the climb up. He grunted, groaned and puffed. He mumbled, moaned and puffed. He sweated, swore and puffed. "This stomach of mine is weighing a ton. Being a glutton is hard work," he confessed.

With much stress and strain he won the rim. He sat there, his feet dangling inside the jar and his stomach sagging down on his knees. He studied the remaining cookies, contemplating the possibility of going down for just one more.

"Tomorrow night," he decided, "I'll be cleaning this cookie jar clean as a whistle."

Hardly had he reached the decision when we was attacked by a twisting pang in his overloaded stomach. So sudden and sharp was the pain that it toppled him from the jar. With a jolt that drove the pain from his stomach he landed in a china cup. He tried to scramble to his feet only to find that his tail was snarled around the handle of the cup. He tugged at his tail, and the cup wobbled to the edge of the shelf. He stopped yanking just in time. For seconds the cup teetered on the edge and finally settled to a fine balance. Having gotten himself out, the Imp disentangled his tail and stared wide-eyed at the floor far below.

"That," he exclaimed with a windy whistle, "was brinking on disaster."

He clambered down the front of the kitchen cabinet, and, holding up his belly with his hands, waddled down the hall. Every few feet he paused to groan with the aches of indigestion.

He stumbled through the charcoals of the burned out logs in the grate and attempted to climb up the bricks of the chimney to his cave. His toes and fingers could not touch the bricks simultaneously. His belly held him too far out. In irritation he clapped his middle. "O you nuisance" he addressed his stomach, "you are being in the way like a pocketful of ice!"

The Imp sat down in the corner of the grate and set himself to thinking. All out of sorts he was. He was cross. He crossed his arms; he crossed his legs; he even crossed his eyes.

"I'm cross as two sticks," he declared. "Being a glutton is having pains in the stomach, having roachy dreams, falling out of cookie jars and being locked out of home. In the future I'll be seeing to it that I'm not the biggest glutton in the world. I'm being only a small glutton hereafter."

Gray light pushed against the windowpanes seeking entrance into the house. Morning was ready to awaken the world. In the mother's room the alarm clock triggered off like a pit full of rattlesnakes. The Imp jumped up from the corner of the grate.

"In no timing to speak of," he told himself frantically, "all my enemies will be abroad. Again he tried to scale the chimney wall, but his belly was still in the way. He jumped from the hearth onto the floor and began trotting around the room like a trackman working out. He was a bloated imp trying to work his stomach in. While he ran, his belly bounced down and up like a cork on a fishing line. He stopped under each chair to chin himself six times on each rung. Dawn began to evict the darkness from the corners of the room, and the Imp heard the father stirring. He made a go at the chimney once more. He started up, groaning near to tears. "Now I am being so tired I can hardly climb."

When he was half way up to his cave he paused, clung to the bricks and rested. Over the sound of his own panting he heard noises below; and, looking down, he saw large hands clearing the ashes from the grate. The Imp shuddered at the realization of how close he had come to falling into the hands of his enemy. Finding strength and breath he climbed the remainder of the way and plunged into the security of home. Lying on his back he put his hands under his head.

"Hereafter and for all time," he assured himself, "I am glutting only in my own househole." He patted his stomach. Then he closed his eyes and murmured drowsily: "And now I am calling upon sleep." Sleep came quickly as though all the time it had been waiting as a comforter in the blackness of the cave.

CHAPTER 4

Usually cooks are fat people. Whether they are cooks because they are fat or fat because they are cooks may someday be matter for a Kinsey report. Fat people are, as a rule, jolly people. They are jolly, possibly, because they have always the joyous expectation of the next good thing to eat. While hunger makes for ill humor, a full stomach makes for laughter. To insure a happy day, one should have a hearty breakfast.

The cook in the house where dwelt the Impulsive Imp was thin as a rail. Her heart was cold as a gravedigger's feet and her bones seemed bursting out all over. Any cook so thin must have had six duodenal ulcers or a persisting dislike of her own cooking. This cook was not a jolly cook; and that was sure as grits are groceries. Her name was Septuagesima.

When Septuagesima entered the kitchen the sun seemed trying to push all its light through the kitchen window.

"Drat it," said she, "it's enough to blind a soul."

She reached for the string to pull down the shade only to discover that shade and string were wrapped out of reach around the stick.

"Drat it," she repeated, "what meddling Tom did that?"

She told herself that before she went to the garage for the stepladder she would have her spot of tea and cookies. Her brow became ruffled as a windswept sea when she found the kitchen cabinet door swung wide. "Now look at this," she complained, "open to the roaches. Drat it all! They've made a playground of my kitchen."

Having brewed her tea she reached into the cookie jar; and a storm began to brew for Alan and Alice. "As I live," she cried, "only three cookies left. And a roach besides! Drat them kids. I'll speak my mind about this. Last night the jar was half full, and they know I only take a cup of tea and a cookie for breakfast. They take all but three and then leave the cloth off so a roach can get in to spoil them three!"

Since she could have no cookie, Septuagesima poured the tea down the drain. Perhaps she did not know that some children were starving. Perhaps she knew but didn't care. The failure to have her tea and cookie added much to her bad temper. Anyone who pours good tea down a drain simply for lack of a cookie has a bad temper not only in word but in deed. Septuagesima slammed down the frying pan on the stove and began preparing the bacon and eggs for the family's breakfast.

The mother heard the banging in the kitchen and said to the father: "Seppy must be in a temper again."

"I hope not too bad a temper," replied he, "or the eggs will give me indigestion."

"No one gets indigestion from eggs," she told him.

"It isn't just plain eggs that give me indigestion," the father explained, "it's burnt eggs."

"Maybe she won't burn the toast," the mother was optimistic.

"Septuagesima doesn't have to be in a temper to burn the toast," he asserted. "Why do we keep her?"

"She isn't a bad person at heart."

"Naturally not—she has no heart."

"Sh-h-h-h," the mother warned. "She might hear you, and it's almost impossible to get a cook. Besides, the children might hear you."

"Are they both up?" he asked.

"Yes, saying their morning prayers."

Alice, being a barefaced appetite going under the likeness of a girl, was the first to reach the kitchen. Alan, with homework on his mind, straggled behind her. He was polishing his shoe on the leg of his trousers. He stopped abruptly when he felt on him the stern eye of Septuagesima.

"There was only a little dust on 'em." He mitigated the polishing.

"Was there a little dust on the cookies?" asked Seppy sarcastically.

"On what cookies?" asked Alan.

"On what cookies?" echoed Alice.

"On the jar full of cookies I made yesterday. The cookies you two stole!"

"No we didn't," Alan declared. "We never steal anything."

"It's a naughty thing to steal," stated Alice. "And when anyone talks like that to me I cry." Therewith she began to weep in no uncertain terms.

The mother hastened into the kitchen. "Why the tears, Alice?" she asked.

"Seppy called us thieves," sobbed Alice, "and thieves die on crosses, and I don't want to die on a cross. Neither Alan."

"Seppy says we been at the cookies," Alan elucidated.

The mother told Alice to go to the bathroom to bathe her eyes. Alice said it wouldn't do any good because once she started crying she couldn't stop. The mother informed her that weeping would not be allowed in the kitchen before breakfast.

"Any now, Seppy," the mother asked, "Why do you say the children have been at the cookie jar?"

"Look!" And Seppy showed her the contents of the jar. "The cloth was off the top this morning, and yesterday I baked a fresh batch."

The mother instructed Seppy to empty out the roach and three cookies, and to put the jar in the sink to be scalded. She asked the father if he had eaten the cookies.

"Not a one," he responded emphatically.

The mother sighed and asked Seppy if she were sure that she had made cookies just the day before. Seppy, lifting her eyes to heaven in long suffering, proclaimed she was positive the jar had been almost full.

"Then Alan," decided the mother, "you and Alice must have eaten them."

"But I didn't. I tell you, I didn't."

"Me neither," cried Alice. "I can't reach the jar."

"Only you two like Seppy's cookies well enough to eat a whole jar full," the father interjected.

"But we didn't eat 'em." Alan was growing sullen under the accusations.

"Thief first and then liar," snapped Septuagesima.

"You mustn't speak to the children like that," the mother interposed. "There are no thieves or liars in this house!"

She, of course, was unaware of the Impulsive Imp sleeping blissfully in his cave.

"Someone must have eaten the cookies," Seppy persisted.

"Maybe you ate 'em yourself." Alan took the offensive.

"Myself! Myself!" she ejaculated. "I didn't even have one to go with my tea."

"I'm sorry, Seppy," said the mother, "but let's drop the matter now. I'll speak to the children after breakfast."

"By all means," the father concurred, "let's postpone everything 'til after breakfast. Bring me my hatchet, and let's get on with the eggs."

Breakfast finished, the mother spoke to Alan before he set out for school.

"You and Alice are punished today. I want you to come home immediately after school."

"But mother—" he began to protest.

"No interruptions, please. You will spend the evening at your schoolbooks. Alice will stay in the house all day, and she may not play with Susan. In the future if you want anything, ask."

"I didn't take those darn cookies."

"If you didn't take them," said the mother, "I am punishing you unjustly, and you must forgive me. If you did take them, you deserve a greater punishment for saying that you didn't."

"But if I didn't take 'em, why are you punishing me at all?" he complained. "I don't want to be punished unjustly or any other way. And I don't want to have to forgive you."

"That will be all." The mother hustled him out. "You'll be late for school."

Alice took her punishment with good grace. She played in the house all day, and, on the whole, behaved well. Of course, she made a shambles of the living room. She lined the chairs up as a train, using the study-table as a locomotive. With the cushions from the studio couch she erected a tunnel and drove the train through it a chair at a time. The locomotive, however, was too heavy to move. She punished her dolls, making each sit in a corner. Having one more corner than dolls, she sat herself there and wrote on the wall with a green crayon. The mother discovered her about to test the red crayon on the wall. Alice remained in the corner; the crayons went with the mother.

At least five times during the day the mother regretted having restricted Alice to the house. Confinement enlarged her appetite until it could have taken the measure of a wolf. Every fifteen minutes or so she sought out the mother to beg an apple, an orange or a piece of bread and jelly.

"Go ask Seppy," the mother advised her.

"I will not disturve Seppy," she asserted. "I rather for you to give it to me."

"Seppy won't mind."

"She gives me the smallest apple," claimed Alice. "and I can't taste the jelly when she puts it on the bread."

"You mustn't dislike Seppy."

"I didn't say I didn't like her," Alice countered. "It's her who don't like me. She just don't like little girls. Little boys neither."

"You shouldn't say unkind things. You must like someone in order to have someone like you." The mother's voice grew stern.

"Kin I have an apple?" Alice evaded the issue.

From breakfast to lunch, from lunch to dinner, with oranges and apples to help the hours, the day passed. Alan came home from school and forced his nose into his books. For once he was not reluctant to accede to Alice's request that he read to her from his Second Grade Reader.

The father came in from work. On his coat collar and shoulders lay flakes of feathery snow fast dissolving.

"Hello, scholars," he called into the breakfast room where Alan was reading *Our New Friends* to Alice. "Could I wheedle a buss on the cheek?"

Alice jumped up. "Let me kiss first so I can feel the outside of your face. Listen, Daddy," she rushed on after brushing his cheek, "Alan and me's been punished all day."

"A miscarriage of justice, no doubt."

"We didn't take the cookies," Alan again pleaded his innocence.

"Plump no," affirmed Alice.

"My knuckle-headed defendants," he said, discarding his topcoat, "let me state the case. The plaintiff, one Septuagesima, charges that last night a jar almost full of cookies stood on the kitchen cabinet shelf. This morning said jar was nigh empty. One roach, apprehended at the scene of the crime, is an accessory after the fact, which means that he couldn't have eaten all those cookies. Mother didn't eat them. I wouldn't, and the plaintiff claims she didn't even have one to go with her tea. Neither of you touched the cookies; therefore, Alice, you tell me: who ate those cookies?"

"I'm Alice," said Alice, "and I didn't eat 'em."

"It's too bad you can't be more impersonal about the confounded pastry," said the father, "but all right, you didn't eat them. So Alan, you tell me, who ate the cookies."

"I guess nobody must of ate them."

"Not too scholarly put, but clear," agreed the father. "A jar full of cookies which no one ate but which, nevertheless, were all eaten up."

"Maybe a rat," suggested Alan.

"Hardly. How would it have gotten in and out of the jar."

"Maybe a ghost," Alice made a try.

"The most sensible explanation so far," stated the father, "but I've yet to see a cookie-eating ghost. In fact, I've yet to see a ghost, thank goodness."

"Then, who?" asked Alan.

"Yes, who?" echoed Alice.

"Thereon, my little owls, hangs the mystery. You two figure it out while I have dinner."

"Could you light the logs in the living room?" Alan requested.

"Yep. It's a night for logs, and a grate fire goes with Sherlocking." The father lighted the logs and, leaving Alan and Alice, heads close together sitting on the rug by the hearth, he went seeking the mother and dinner.

CHAPTER 5

When the logs were set afire in the grate the smoke billowed up the chimney. To the nose of the Impulsive Imp it arose like incense. He sniffed, working his nose like a loose button. He opened his eyes and sleep ran away. His first impulse was to race down the chimney and make for the cookie jar. Remembering his blistered tail, he held himself in check. When he poked his head out of the cave, he saw the flames dancing and sword fighting far below.

"So ho, where there is being smoke there is being fire."

He wrapped his tail close around his waist. Kissing the tip, he tucked it inside the coil. Slowly he descended. As he neared the opening of the grate he heard the sound of voices.

"I am having enemies on the loose," muttered he, "enemies and more so. I guess I am having more enemies than anybody else in the whole world."

He came to rest on the narrow ledge that jutted out on the inside of the chimney just above the fireplace. Almost all the old chimneys have such a ledge. Many precious things have been hidden on such ledges, and chimney sweeps have sometimes become rich men. The Imp found nothing precious. He found much soot, however, that made a soft cushion on which to lie. Lying there he felt very smug and sly, because he could hear every word spoken in the living room.

"How do you start unraving a mystery?" he heard Alice ask.

"You got to get fingerprints," Alan replied.

"Whose fingerprints do you gotta get?"

"The one who took the cookies."

"How we gonna get 'em when we don't know who took the cookies?"

"I wish you'd get older in a hurry," said Alan impatiently, "so you'd understand things."

"I'm Alice," said Alice, "and I understand all about fingerprints. I make 'em on the walls and doors."

"Well, don't ask silly questions."

"If you talk to your little sister like that" Alice informed him, "I'm not going to unrave a mystery with you."

"Daddy gives us a job to do, and you don't cooperate," Alan accused her.

"I will, too, if you'll tell me what's next."

"Well, you get fingerprints," Alan continued, "and you send 'em off to the F.B.I."

"What's the F.B. high?"

"Gee whiz!" exclaimed Alan, "If you'd listen to *Gang Busters* sometimes 'stead of running out the room when the machine gun starts, you'd know about the F.B.I."

"I don't like gang bustin'," Alice informed him. "I don't like any kind of bustin'."

"I'd like to know how you're ever gonna be a detective." Alan was disgusted.

"You know what?" Alice's voice sank confidentially. "I betcha a dollar and a half Seppy took the cookies."

"How do you know?"

"She don't like us. She just wanted to get us punished."

"You ought not say that." Alan glanced over his shoulder. "But I bet you're right."

"And you know what else?"

"Now don't you make anything up," Alan warned her.

"I'm Alice, and I'm not making anything up." She was insulted, but not so much so as to withhold her knowledge. "Seppy made some more cookies today, and she found a key for the kitchen cabinet, and she's gonna lock the kitchen cabinet tonight and keep the key around her neck."

The Impulsive Imp almost fell off the ledge when he heard Alice recount Seppy's plan. He sprang to his feet, clenched his fists, gnashed his teeth and marched up and down the ledge. He strained to do battle. Bethinking himself he pulled up short to hear what else his enemies had to say.

"Seppy is a mean cook," Alan averred. "I'll never eat any more of her cookies even if she makes 'em out of pure gold."

"Me neither!" Alice was in complete concurrence.

"Let's make a promise," Alan proposed. He crooked his little finger and Alice crooked hers. They hooked their fingers together and held them so linked while Alan spoke the words of the promise.

"We'll never, never eat any more of Seppy's cookies until frogs turn into grasshoppers. If I ever eat her cookies I hope I turn into a frog. If you ever eat her cookies you hope you turn into a grasshopper."

"I'd rather become mice," said Alice.

"You mean 'a mouse.'"

"No. I want to be more than one," she insisted, "so I'll have somebody to play with."

CHAPTER 6

The Impulsive Imp was confronted with a dilemma. He had no liking for it, possibly because it had horns. Should he go without cookies or should he beard his Seppy in her den? Bulls, billy goats, rhinoceroses, dilemmas: horns to beware of.

"She is cutting me off from my supply of food," mused the Imp, "and starving me into starvation. I am taking this dilemma by the horns and throwing it at her head."

For hours he lay on the sooty couch of the ledge and turned the matter over in his mind. The situation looked black as the wall of the chimney. Long after Alice and Alan had been tucked into bed he still struggled on the horns of the dilemma. The logs had burned out, and a cold draft swept past him up the flue. The Imp shivered.

"Things are getting blacker by the minutes," he said. "I'm in a fitting temper to be declaring war on this cook called Seppy."

He hooked his tail on the ledge and lowered himself. The cinders crunched a little under his puny weight. Standing on the hearth he gnashed his teeth into the room. His teeth chattered with chill; for the temperature had fallen outside. The room was colder than it had been the night before. He leaped out onto the rug, stumbled over Alice's dolls and fell. His hair stood up and his flesh prickled over his body as he found himself face to face, sprawling on top of what he was sure was one of his enemies.

Quivering with ferocity born of fear he swung his fist down upon his enemy's nose. He yelped with the pain that stabbed through his knuckles, while the doll's enameled nose suffered no damage. The Imp sat on the doll's chest and nursed the bruise.

"I am almost breaking my hand in six places, but I guess I am killing this enemy mightily dead." Standing up he prodded the doll with his toe. "Now he's being dead as Caesar, I'm taking myself the spoils of war."

He removed the blue, knitted, turtleneck sweater from the doll and pulled it on over his head. The knitted, knee-length trousers were a snug fit, but caused his tail to stand up straight along his back.

"This will never be doing," he said, studying the barb dangling over his head. "It looks like a trolley that's jumping the wire." Twisting the pantaloons, so that he could reach the rear, he remedied the matter by pulling the woolen mesh open sufficiently to allow the barb and tail to slip through. "There," he spoke with satisfaction, "my tail is not only getting in the proper place, but it is also holding up these pretty pants. I guess I'm being the most ingenious imp in the whole world."

The hall clock chimed the hour of one, and the Imp bethought himself of his stomach. His mouth began to water as he recalled the flavor of the cookies. He also began to simmer with anger in the recollection that Septuagesima had effectively barred him from the jar.

"I will be biting this Seppy cook on all her toes, one by one," he determined. "I'm in a fitting temper to be declaring war on this malicious foe."

On the rung of the rocking chair he chinned himself eleven times to make sure he was limber. While he chinned he conjectured: "Maybe this Seppy cook is being littler than me, and I am beating the stew out of her." He gave the chair a kick and it commenced to rock. "One of these days I am getting some other imps and selling them tickets to ride on this rocker; but now I'm not having time. I am having a war on my hands."

Therewith the Imp set out in search of Septuagesima. In the first bedroom he found Alice. She lay in an old fashioned bed with scrollwork on the head and foot of it. Its corner posts were thick at the top and tapered at the bottom with vine leaves carved upon them. On each leaf was wrought a cherub's head whose eyes drooped with sleep. The Imp perched on a corner post and looked down with wonder on the little girl. She lay with her face on her hand. Her hair washed out around her head. Her cheek, pressed against the back of her hand, caused her lips to part in a cupid's bow. The Imp put his elbow on his knee and rested his chin in his hand.

"This is not being a stupid cook," he mused. "This is being no other than a princess having hair like spun gold, pretty as fairy wings. Some day I am figuring out how she can be so pretty while I am being so ugly. Maybe she could be liking me even though I am being an ugly imp with a heart as black as the soles of my feet. I guess nobody could be liking the ugliest imp in the whole world."

Wallowing in self-pity the Imp closed his eyes. Two tears were squeezed out from between the lids. They were tiny as the drops of dew on the petal of a rose. He lowered himself into the bed and, lifting some of Alice's hair, let it slide between his fingers.

"It is being silky as silk," he whispered. He pressed the hair against his cheek. Then he stretched himself out on the hair that was like a pool around Alice's head. "This is being a kingly couch," he sighed and would have fallen asleep; but

Alice stirred in her sleep. He scurried across the bed and slid down the post.

"If she is seeing me, she is screaming like the house is in a conflageration." He looked back over his shoulder before quitting the room. "I'm coming back to see this pretty each night of the week," he avowed. "I am loving her like fairies are loving their queen."

In the next room the Imp found Alan. He was rolled up like a doodlebug under the blankets.

"Nor is this being a cook," said the Imp. "This is being a boy, and boys have more imp in them than I am having in me. If he catches me, he is tying tomato cans to my tail, no doubting."

He slipped quietly through the nearest door to find himself in the bathroom that separated Alan's from Alice's bedroom. A razor blade gleamed like a cat's eye on the floor behind the clothes hamper. Startled, he nevertheless approached it cautiously and picked it up.

"This is being a mean weapon." Striking a pose, his right foot forward and his left slightly behind, he brandished the blade like a sword. He whipped it up and down, back and forth, and around like a flail. "Be on guarding, old Seppy cook, for the greatest swordsimp in the whole world." He made a stab at the bathtub and sliced at the clothes hamper. Resting the blade on his shoulder, he marched out of the bathroom, intoning as he took up his search: "I am looking for Goliath. I am looking for Goliath!"

The Impulsive Imp skirted the bedroom of the father. The previous night's experience had taught him to have no further "truck" with the father who was responsible for his hair-raising, tail-smacking ride on the shade. He did, however, pause in the alcove to admire his new suit and to practice before the mirror the use of his sword. He thrust and drove and made murderous slashes. He swayed from the hip, rose on his toes and rocked on his heels. Planting his foot on an imaginary foe he had slain, he bowed with a flourish of his blade to his image in the mirror.

"I am being a holy terror," he boasted. "Wait 'til I'm coming up with this Seppy cook."

In the kitchen he climbed up and verified that the doors of the kitchen cabinet were locked. "The spun-golden girl is right. This Seppy cook has been finding herself a key."

At the further end of the kitchen a flight of stairs mounted into a dim light. To the Imp the steps were as formidable as mountains.

"I am not doubting that up there is the stronghold of my greatest enemy," he pronounced, "but I can't be wasting my time and exhausting my strength scaling these mountains." He wound his tail around his waist and thrust the blade inside the coil. Leaping he caught the edge and gained the surface of the bottom step. He then shinnied up a banister to the rail and, using hands and feet, he ascended the balustrade with the agility of a monkey. At the top he swung down onto the landing under the dim light.

The door to Septuagesima's room was ajar. That fact raised some doubt in the Imp's mind as to the existence of the door; for how can a door be a door when it is ajar. He did not stop to ponder the incongruity. In he went. Having come by a sword, he was behooved to subject impulse to strategy. By means of the knobs he climbed to the top of the chest of drawers in order to study the terrain over which he would attack. Confronting himself in another mirror, serious operations were suspended again while he practiced a thrust and a parry. He spun off a pirouette for good measure and, satisfied with his increasing ability as a swordsimp, he set himself to examine his archenemy.

breaking bounds. After a few seconds, gaining a mite of calm, he gathered in his tail and coiled it beside him.

"This is a kettle of fishing like nothing is ever before," he muttered in desperation.

He decided to lie still until the cook would change her position again, and so release him. Thirty seconds had not passed before he became the most impatient imp in the whole world. Each second lingered as though it had no place to go. The stillness of the room rang in his ears. Then he was appalled by the realization that she might move in the wrong direction. He would be crushed.

"This monstrous monster," he exclaimed, "is first putting me in stocks. Now she is getting ready to mash me gristings in the mill. I can't be staying in her stockings any longer."

He picked up the coil of his tail and tossed it at Seppy. She did not move.

"It is needing more heaviness," he decided. Taking his tail he tied three knots in its end and tossed it at Seppy's nose. She brushed at her face and rolled over upon her back. As soon as she began to move, the Imp jerked himself away. Jerking too violently he hurled himself over the side of the bed. He sat on the floor, and was as shaken up as a bottle of cough syrup.

The Imp set himself to take the knots out of his tail. Two came out freely, but the third proved stubborn. He pulled at it. He pressed in the tail at each side of the knot. He made faces at it and beat it upon the floor.

"This is being no less than a Gordian knot," he groaned. "But if I am cutting his knot with my sword I will be losing the best part of my tail. An imp that is having no barb on his tail is an Imp whose tale is ending."

He endeavored to undo the knot with his teeth. It remained fast. Ultimately he knew but one thing to do. Hooking the barb of the tail to the bedpost he pulled with all his might to draw the knot tight. Tightening, of course, made the knot smaller.

"At least I am having the use of my tail," he sighed, "but I am knotted for life."

It might be thought that after his narrow escape the Imp would have returned to the security of his cave. A less intrepid imp might have sought something other than cookies to eat. But the Impulsive Imp set out again, undaunted, to get the key from around Septuagesima's throat. Again he ascended the bedpost. Hooking his barb to the edge of the quilt at Seppy's neck, he heaved the quilt down to her chest.

"Now," he gloated, "her chest will be getting as cold as her heart."

He unhooked the barb, recovered his sword and climbed to Seppy's chest. He descended into the valley at the base of her throat to look for the key. He found it. The key was attached to a chain that a razor blade could never sever.

CHAPTER 7

For once the Impulsive Imp did not succumb to a temptation. He did not slash Septuagesima's throat. Instead, he stood on her chest and studied her face.

"You are being the unkindest cook in the whole world," he addressed her bony nose. "If I am not being afraid of waking you, I am twisting off both your ears."

Gloom descended upon him as he climbed down the bedpost. Dejectedly he dragged the handkerchief of booty over the threshold and out of the room. At the head of the steps he hooked his tail into the knot of the bundle; and, climbing to the rail, he slid down, pulling his spoils after him. At the bottom he rested.

"How am I bearing this booty to my cave if I am not having strength to lift it?" He shook his head sadly. "I am being on the verge of famine and full of gloom. If I am full of cookies as I am of gloom, I am being a glutton all over again."

He tested his declining strength. He gripped the handkerchief and found he could lift it.

"This, no doubting, is possible," he said, "because I am being the Herculean imp I am. Having a stomach full of cookies, I am making Atlas small stuffings. Then I am putting two worlds on my back, one over each shoulder, and running myself a short marathon. Then I am being indeed a marvelous imp."

He bore his booty into the kitchen. Glowering at the kitchen cabinet, he half regretted not having taken a slice at the cook's scrawny neck. He looked around the room. Above the refrigerator a shelf was built out from the wall, and on the shelf were stacked a dozen or more small cardboard boxes. The Imp lowered his bundle to the floor.

"If I am having my righteous strength, I would be climbing up there. Maybehaps the boxes are having something in them to eat."

He looked more closely at the little containers. Possibly it was a hungry imp's intuition that led him. He tossed his tail through the handle on the refrigerator door and pulled himself up. From the handle he threw his tail to the top of the refrigerator, and from there to the shelf.

"If ever I am growing up, I will be a fireman on the hook-and-ladder truck."

With his sword he cut a hole in the side of one of the boxes. Through it a stream of light pellets poured out. The Imp sniffed at them.

"They are smelling not bad," he commented. "I will be finding out what my stomach is thinking of them."

He reached for one of the pellets. Thinking it would be heavy as it appeared to be, he took it with a tight grasp. It crunched and crackled in his hand. Looking wide-eyed at the bits he marveled:

"I am not knowing my own strength. Even in my weakness I am being the strongest imp in the whole world."

Delicately he picked up another pellet. It melted on his tongue. Pellet after pellet he thrust into his mouth. A feeling of well being pervaded him, dispersing the pall of gloom. He licked his lips as the high-water mark of his stomach was reached.

"Before my appetite is all going I will be sampling some more of these boxes." He cut holes in the sides of three other boxes, and streams of like pellets issued from all. "If these puff balls and cookies are all my enemies are eating," he decided, "they will be suffering dietary deficiencies. When their legs are all bending with rackets, I am cutting them down like wheaties."

Next to the small boxes was a large white bag. Sated with the pellets, the Imp decided to sample its contents. From the slash made by his sharp blade came a white flood, and he cupped his hands and tasted.

"It is being sweet like sugar," he exclaimed. "and when it is coming to sugar, I am being a regulation elephant with a large tooth."

The sound of crunching, steady crunching, came to the Imp's ear. For a moment or so he attached no importance to it. Then a thought stole upon him and interrupted his gourmandizing as though with a tap on the shoulder. "That crunching is not being sugar melting in your mouth," the thought warned him. "Melting does not make crunching."

"Which is being right as a stoplight," the Imp agreed. "Melting does not make crunching."

"If melting is not crunching," the thought persisted, "What is making the crunching?"

The Imp withdrew his lips from the slit in the bag, and shoved in his fingers to dam the flow of sugar. He stood still as a totem pole and listened. The crunching continued. Without turning he peeped from the corner of his eye. His hair stood up and seemed to him to be walking around on his head. Two mice, which to a small imp might just as well have been two Kodiak bears, were eating the crispy pellets. Their teeth were moving as fast as a sewing machine needle and were just as sharp. Hugging the bag, the Imp tiptoed around it. Feeling somewhat sheltered, he inspected the mice. They were longer than he was tall, and their eyes darted alertly to pick up any movement in any direction.

"They are having as many teeth as band saws." The Imp shuddered. "Enemies they are being no doubting, and thieves for sure."

The Imp considered dashing at them of a sudden and laying upon them with his sword. He might put them both to flight. But what if they stood ground and ripped at him with their pointed teeth?

"I am being most ferocious," the Imp assured himself, "but when I am being outnumbered, desertion is the better part of valor; and it is wiser I am fleeing today to be fighting some other day."

He hurriedly stuck his barb into the shelf and began his descent. In his haste to be fighting some other day, he failed to note beforehand that he was not over the refrigerator; nor had he sunk the barb of his tail securely enough into the shelf. He was half way down his tail when the motor of the refrigerator snapped automatically on. The click and ensuing vibration unnerved him. His chattering indecision as to whether he should flee up or down was abruptly ended, for the barb of his tail flew free and he plummeted toward the floor. As he shot down, he groaned: "I am being an ace number one paratrooper—having no parachute."

The drop terminated with a wee clink, a splash and a snorting. The Imp had landed in the cat's saucer of milk. With his fingers he threw the milk out of his eyes; and he blew milk out of his nose and mouth. He hopped to the floor and regarded himself.

"I am being wet as Monday's wash," he complained, "and white is not becoming me. I am toiling up six feet to fall into a saucer of milk; and before, when I am down here starving, I am finding nothing to eat."

The Imp knelt over the edge of the saucer and slurped what remained of the milk. As he arose from drinking, he glanced up to find the two mice furtively peeping over the edge of the shelf. He stuck his tongue out at them.

"Someday," he told them, "I will be whipping the stew-meat out of you like David is whipping Goliath."

The mice rolled up their lips at him. He quickly shouldered his bundle of loot, and went trudging down the hall.

CHAPTER 8

I t might be thought, from what is known of the Imp, that he was a wicked imp. Impulsive and wicked are not the same, although impulsiveness often results in acts that appear to be wicked. To be too quick to judge an act wicked is to be an impulsive judge; and it is far better to be impulsively charitable than to be an impulsive judge. Charity should extend far, falling short only of Septuagesima. She did not like children.

When the sun gripped the horizon and pulled itself up, Septuagesima slid from beneath the blankets. She claimed she was always up with the sun. It is to be doubted that the sun felt honored.

The light was not bright in the room when the cook looked at herself in the mirror above the chest of drawers. She uttered a small shriek. Septuagesima had reason to shriek any time she looked into a mirror, but this morning she had additional reason. Her face appeared streaked with white. Septuagesima claimed she was no "namby-pamby" who went about fainting like other women; hence she did not faint when she saw her face painted like that of a Tchoupitoulas Indian. She rubbed her cheeks with her hands. Nothing came off on her fingers. She turned on the light to examine her face more closely. She saw then that the mirror and not her face was streaked.

"Children!" she snarled, and her mouth twisted up the side of her face. "Devils and rascals. Drat the miscreants!"

Snatching up the comb, Septuagesima went at her hair. The comb dragged. She yanked it out and saw that it was smeared with cold cream. She was fit to be tied—and with nothing lighter than anchor chain. She swelled with anger. Her cheeks puffed out like the neck of a lizard.

"I'll murder them kids!" she exploded.

After a moment, however, cunning entered her face. She would hold her peace, be clever like a fox, set snares and entrap Alan and Alice at their wrongdoing. Down the steps she went softly. She was on her way to examine Alan's hands. She would surprise him with the cold cream still on his fingers or under his nails. As she crossed the kitchen floor she set up a crunching and crackling like six girls eating peanuts at a movie. From the larger white bag the sugar was still spilling in a tittering stream.

"Next they'll be doing me bodily harm, them angels," she sneered. "Reared in disrespect and irresponsibility," she muttered as she turned the sugar bag on its side to stop the flow. "Bound to be juvenile delinquents, that's what they'll be. Cereal all over the floor. Sugar! The cat's milk splattered. The little vandals! Drat their souls!"

Septuagesima found no cold cream on Alan's fingers. There was only a little ingrained dirt that is one with a boy. On her blankets Alice's hands were plump and clean. Septuagesima told herself that already they were accomplished criminals who cleaned their hands after their crimes.

The mother found Septuagesima as cold as ice and almost as uncommunicative. The cereal had been swept into a neat heap in the center of the kitchen floor. It looked like a little grave under which lay buried the night's wrongdoings. If the cereal was a grave, Seppy's face was a headstone. Dire happenings were written all over it, and it gave welcome to nothing but misfortune. While she prepared breakfast her silence was as disturbing as kettledrums. The mother, in the interest of the father's eggs, said nothing until the frying was done.

"You're quiet this morning, Seppy," the mother ventured.

"Quiet breeds no trouble, Ma'am."

"There's something to be said for that," the mother agreed pleasantly, "but you need have no fear of breeding trouble."

"Perhaps not, Ma'am."

"Is there something wrong?"

"Not a thing—with me," Seppy replied coldly, and she walked across the kitchen taking care to step on the heap of cereal that crackled angrily under foot.

"You seem to have spilled some cereal," the mother remarked.

Septuagesima turned and looked at her. All the grievous wrong done woman since Eve was historied on the cook's face.

"I humbly beg your pardon," she said, half closing her eyes with the pain of accusation, "but I did not spill anything on the floor."

"But that is cereal," the mother insisted innocently.

"I did not spill it." It was a flat, hard statement.

"Oh," said the mother in a small voice, "I wonder who did."

Alan and Alice, like unknowing lambs, came in to be slaughtered. Seppy looked upon them with eyes like flails. The mother's eyes were puzzled under a frown.

"Did you two spill the cereal?"

"What cereal?" they asked in unison.

The mother vaguely rubbed her temple. "There's something funny here."

"Three boxes with holes punched in them. A ten-pound bag of sugar cut open. Is that funny, Ma'am?" Seppy cruelly pushed the business.

"I'm Alice," flared Alice, "and I didn't punch holes in no boxes. In the sugar bag neither."

"In *any* boxes," the father corrected as he entered the kitchen. "What tribulation fills the land this morning?"

"Holes punched in things," said Alan with disgust, "and I betcha Alice and me are gonna get punished again."

"Never mind," the mother cut short the discussion, "We'll talk about it after breakfast."

The family ate in silence. Septuagesima sucked her thin lips.

The father had brushed his teeth, set his hat at a satisfactorily jaunty angle, and was ready to depart for work. When a man is dressed, fed and ready for work, he is impatient to be off. If his wife detains him, he will fidget. He pats his pockets to assure himself that he has not forgotten his handkerchief, his keys, his pen. He begins to be tormented by termite doubts. Did he bring some papers home the night before? Was it three mornings he had been late in the past week?

"These happenings are getting serious," the mother told him.

"Pranks," he replied, "childish pranks."

"Eating the cookies, maybe, was a prank," she said, "but to willfully punch holes in three boxes of cereal and waste sugar—I don't think that's a prank."

"Mischief," he explained nervously. "Children go off on tangents now and then. Retaliation for being punished. Child psychology. Don't be harsh with them."

The mother bridled. "I've never been harsh with them."

"I know, dear. I know you haven't." He kissed down her ruffled feathers. "It's getting late; I must leave."

"It isn't the things they've done that bother me so much," she disregarded his impatience. "But they deny having done them."

"Self-preservation," he said knowingly.

"It's lying!"

"But they've never lied before," he defended them.

"Well, they've started now; and we have to do something about it. What do you suggest?"

"Sell Septuagesima down the river."

"Go to work. You're more help there."

"Gladly!" He kissed her and ran.

Alan had predicted correctly. He and Alice were punished again. Alice was not allowed to play with her favorite bride-doll, Mary Jane. She was permitted to play in the back yard, where she bullied the cat; but every few minutes she came in to console Mary Jane. She shoved out her lower lip and gave sympathetic regard to Mary Jane, who sat with her soiled, bridal gown billowed about her. Mary Jane's head hung at a broken-neck angle.

"Alice will take you for a long walk tomorrow," she promised Mary Jane. "Alice will rock you all day and sing you to sleep. It's nice for you to be punished with me; but, remember, mother punished you. I won't never punish you no matter what you do."

Alice made one valiant effort to circumvent her mother. She plotted what seemed a reasonable plot.

"Mother," she began confidently, "Mary Jane needs exercise."

"Not today, she doesn't."

"If she sits in the corner all today, if Mary Jane don't get some walking, she will get some awful consipation."

"I don't think she will," said the mother.

"Mary Jane thinks you're the most unkindest grandmother she's got."

"You must explain to Mary Jane why you're punished," prompted the mother, "then she won't think I'm unkind."

"I can't esplain it to her," cried Alice, throwing out her hands in childish desperation. "I can't even esplain it to me."

"Kindly go out in the yard and play," the mother told her.

"All right," Alice gave in, "but if Mary Jane gets consipated, will you give me some Milk of Magic tablets for her?"

The mother said she would; and Alice, satisfied with having carried one point, went out again to play.

That evening Alan and Alice put their heads together in consideration of the sad state of affairs.

"I don't understand Mother and Daddy," Alan mourned.

"Me neither," Alice sighed.

"It's a bad thing in a boy's life when his parents don't believe him anymore."

"They don't believe me neither," Alice pointed out.

"It isn't so bad for girls," Alan claimed, "'cus nobody expects much of a girl; but a boy has to be a man."

"I got to be a man, too," Alice expostulated.

"You can't be a man."

"If I never tell a lie and don't cry when I scrape my knees, I can be jus' as good as a man."

"I'm Alice," she continued, "and I can be as good as any man. And if you say I can't, I won't ever speak to you once more."

"You see," Alan said resignedly, "we're even fighting with each other. You know what?"

"What?"

"You and me are going to get complexes."

"What's complexes?" Alice managed the word.

"Things nobody ought to have. Like pneumonia and whooping cough."

"I don't want any."

"Me neither," said Alan. "Maybe we ought to get Mother and Daddy to see a spychiatrist."

CHAPTER 9

The Impulsive Imp awakened. He had been asleep only a few hours. He blinked his eyes, for a shaft of sunlight had probed down the chimney and was exploring his face.

"It is being most impolite for the sun to be waking me up in the middle of my sleep," he grumbled. "I will be getting a shade for my cave."

He turned his face away from the sunlight and endeavored to entice sleep to return. With his eyes closed, he breathed exactly fourteen times a minute. Sleep did not come. Beginning with his toes, he tried to relax all the muscles of his puny body. Instead of relaxing, his muscles tautened; and he developed a knot in his left calf. He counted cookies rolling down a hill until they added up to eight thousand. Sleep, however, had abandoned the cave.

"By Georging," he snorted, "this is doing nothing but making me a mattressmatician." He sat up. "I guess I am having the best case of insomnia in the whole world."

He sat at the edge of his cave and dangled his legs down the chimney. He realized he was being a most foolish imp to be quitting his bed when the world was infested with his enemies awake. He growled to himself: "I am getting into the most unhumorous humor. Maybe it's because I am getting up on the wrong side of the chimney."

Soon he tired of looking down at the cold grate; and there came upon him, as there comes upon every boy, girl or imp at some time or another, an imperative urge to explore. This urge is manifest in the little girl who explores her mother's cedar-chest, in the little boy who explores his nose. The Imp did what he had never done before. Instead of climbing down, he climbed up the chimney. Up and up he toiled until he was rewarded with a new world. Suddenly, over his head was a mushroom of sky.

"Who-o-o-o-o! Who-o-o-ing" he fittingly exclaimed.

He rubbed his eyes because the glare of the sunlight on the snow blinded him. As far and away as he could see, the world was white. The roof, snow covered, slanted down from the chimney.

"I am knowing now what a little imp I am being," he said with awe. "But some one of these days I will be building me a pair of skis and go shooting down this roof. They will be begging me to go to Switzerland to be showing my stuff."

He gaped at the trees that were all armed with daggers of icicles. He listened to the automobiles sloshing along the streets. In the distance the hills were like a football team of giant snowmen in a huddle.

"It was unknownst to me that I am living in so large a world," he breathed, and inspiration sought him out. "If I am having a good subject, I am Shakespearing on the spot."

He closed his eyes tight and pushed the palms of his hands against his cheeks. Of a sudden he broke into song. His singing was melodious, but hardly louder than a whisper down a well.

Pinocchio had a wooden head.
He had a wooden pillow
On his little wooden bed.
He went to sleep,
And he dreamed all night;
And in his dream

He screamed in fright,
For there landed on his head
A hungry termite:
It was a mitemare!

The Imp pursed his lips in satisfaction. "I guess I'm being about the most talented imp in the whole white world." He heard lilting laughter then; and, looking down, he saw Alice in the yard at the back of the house. She was throwing snowballs at the gatepost.

Gladness filled the Imp like bubbles running up the front of a jukebox. "Why, it is being the princess who is laughing like little bells on a Christmas sleigh. It is joy to an ugly imp to be seeing her again. I am loving her like a dog is loving the moon."

He found contentment standing on the rim of the chimney, watching Alice cup the snow in her hands. When she sent a snowball true to the post, she danced in triumph. The Imp, in company, danced up and down on the rim of the chimney. Twice his tail coiled between his legs, tripping him and almost toppling him down the chimney.

"We are having a glorious time," he shouted. "One time sometime I will be singing my song to her, and she will be my friend."

A voice broke in upon the dancing and put an abrupt end to the snowball throwing. It was Septuagesima calling from the kitchen door. She told Alice to come inside and to come immediately before all the winter swept into the house. The Imp gnashed his teeth. "She is like thistles sticking in my throat. She is having a voice that is sharpening knives."

When Alice went into the house, the world stretching far and away lost its interest. Septuagesima might just as well have reached out and pulled down a shade of darkness. Gladness ran out of the Imp like water running down a drain. With Alice gone, he felt empty as a seashell, lonely as a haunted house. He felt the cold now; he gnashed his teeth and shivered.

"I will be doing dirt like indelible ink to this Seppy cook. She is an enemy like nobody is having an enemy before."

The Impulsive Imp cast discretion to the wind. The wind must be loaded with discretion, since it gets so much cast to it. The Imp was lost against the dark background of the baseboard as he slithered down the hall. Through the alcove he glided and into the kitchen. He did not see Alice, nor was Septuagesima in the kitchen. On the stove a pot, its bottom tickled by the flames, was bubbling with laughter. The Imp crinkled his nose. The odor of food cooking made his nose rumple like a dollar bill in a watch-pocket. Tossing his tail that it caught on the back of the stove, he climbed up. Soup was cooking on the left rear burner. Swirling in the pot, it was red, rich and flecked with gold.

"It is smelling so good," mused the Imp, "I am hardly believing this Seppy cook is making it. I will take a small taste to see if it is good as the smell is bragging."

Impulsively he dipped his finger into the pot. The pain that ran up his arm was so great that, although he opened his mouth, he could not scream. A carpenter might have been driving a row of nails clear up to his shoulder. Worse, by far, was this than a blistered tail. Tears streamed down his cheeks while he shook his finger up and down, hoping it might fly off his hand. Had he a mother to run to it might have been less bad. For a moment he was tempted to run to Alice that her touch might take away some of the hurt. He remembered he was in the land of the enemy, and could only look at his finger and cry.

"I am being a martyr, boiled in soup."

He put his finger into his mouth and sucked away a little of the pain. Then he heard someone descending the stairs at the end of the kitchen. It was Septuagesima coming down from her room. The Imp slid down his tail and hid behind the stove.

The cook ladled up a spoonful of the soup, blew on it and sipped. She smacked her lips uncouthly, and then shook the saltcellar exactly three times over the pot. Peeking around the corner of the stove, the Imp watched her. When she had gone, probably to spy upon the doings of Alice, he climbed up to the top of the stove once more. Putting his tongue to the top of the saltcellar, he licked himself a lick.

"This is not being bad; but too much will be turning the stomach like wind is turning a weather vane."

Twining his legs around the cellar, he gripped the top with both hands. His burned finger throbbed; but he was willing to suffer no little pain to be doing dirt to Septuagesima. The top finally came off, and, dipping his hand again and again into the cellar, he threw salt into the soup. Gleefully he brushed his hands together over the boiling pot.

"This, no doubting, will be shredding the reputation of Seppy cook."

Caution dictated that he return to his cave, but, having prepared the prank, the Imp could not resist the desire to witness its effect. He sought a hiding place and found one secure enough under the refrigerator. There he sat down to wait. Unaccustomed to being abroad during the day, he soon began to yawn, and his third yawn tapered off into sleep.

The afternoon wore into evening while the Impulsive Imp slept. His awakening was violent. A second time the refrigerator motor almost proved his undoing. It went off in his ear like the thunder of an airplane engine. He sprang up and banged his head. Flinging himself down on his stomach, he began to squirm out. Before he was half way out, he twisted frantically and squirmed right back under. The whole family: the mother, father, Alan and Alice were at the table. Septuagesima was serving the soup. The Imp, rubbing his head, peeped upon the scene.

The father, being titular head of the house, was served first. He began to blow upon his soup, but the mother stopped him with a warning eye. Ill-manners! He sat and looked unhappily at his bowl. It was steaming.

"Let us say another Grace Before Meals," he proclaimed. "By then the soup may be cool."

Alice protested: "I said my Grace, and I said it real sweet."

"We will say another Grace, a special Grace for the soup so it will cool especially fast."

"Let me say it." Alice put her palms together and cast down her eyes. "Blessus, O Lord, and these Thy gifts which we are 'bout to receive from Thy country through Christ our Lord, Amen."

"Why does she say *country* instead of *bounty?*" Alan asked the father.

"Why don't you ask me in person instead of just anybody?" Alice complained.

"Well, why do you?"

"'Cus I know what *country* is, and I don't know what *bounty* is. Besides, food comes from the country."

"Daddy, why don't you tell'er what *bounty* is," Alan suggested.

"*Bounty* is something there was mutiny on."

"That isn't what the Catechism teacher told us."

"The soup is now getting cold," the mother told them.

The father took a spoonful of soup into his mouth. He felt his cheeks drawing in. He could not swallow it and, of course, he could not spit it out. He looked at the mother who was about to lift her spoon. He waved his hand, pointed to the soup, pointed to his mouth, and waved his hand again trying to tell her not to take any.

"This is no time for games," she said as she put the spoon to her lips. She and the father looked helplessly at each other and clapped their hands over their mouths.

"What's the matter?" demanded Alan.

"Maybe they were about to say a naughty word," Alice smirked.

The mother arose from the table. She tried to take Alice's bowl.

"Don't take it." Alice clutched the bowl. "I'm not finished. I'm not even started."

The mother could not stop to argue. She dashed after the father out of the kitchen.

When the mother and father returned they found that Alan and Alice had spluttered their soup upon the tablecloth. Septuagesima was roundly reprimanding them.

"They couldn't help it." The mother interrupted her. "The soup is much too salty."

"But I put only a little salt in it."

"Naturally," said the father, "a little barrel of it."

Seppy glared at the father. "Soup has to be a little salty."

"In this instance the salt is a little soupy."

"Don't you like salt?"

"Retail, yes; wholesale, no."

The mother, as usual, was peacemaker. "Seppy just made a little mistake. Anyone who cooks oversalts now and then."

"I beg your pardon." Seppy stood upon her dignity. "I did not salt the soup too much. Three shakes, I tell you; three shakes and no more."

"Taste it, Septuagesima," the mother suggested. "I'm sure you'll agree that it has a little too much salt."

Prepared to make liars of the lot of them, the cook poured some soup. Holding the bowl, she stood over them like a judge. With an expression of longsuffering she took a spoonful of the soup. For one wide-eyed second she retained the soup in her mouth, and then showered it down upon them.

"And *she* scolded *us*," Alice whispered to Alan.

Septuagesima slammed the bowl down upon the table, further staining the cloth. Having wiped her face with her apron, she glowered at the father.

"Someone deliberately ruined my soup. They want me to lose my position. Someone's trying to drive me insane!"

The mother patted Seppy's arm. "It's all right. Please forget about the soup. I'm going to find out about the mysterious things that have been going on in this house."

"Is that mean Alan and me's going to be punished again?" asked Alice.

The mother told her to hush.

Under the refrigerator the Imp rolled with mirth.

"This time for sure I am putting this Seppy cook in the soup!"

CHAPTER 10

Throughout the evening Septuagesima brooded upon the salted soup. The longer she brooded the stronger grew her conviction that it had not been Alan or Alice who spoiled the soup. She began to suspect that the father had emptied the salt cellar into the soup pot. Anyone who had begotten two rapscallions such as Alice and Alan must have bad stuff in him. For the time being she would not expose him to the mother. She would wait until the malefactor had further shown his hand.

For one bleak moment she was attacked by the notion that possibly in such an old house there might be a discontented ghost, a roaming spirit with a weird sense of humor. She gave no welcome to the idea. Better to believe that two villainous children and their haphazard father were the cause of her woe.

Septuagesima set mouse traps. She set them in the places where, she figured, lay the greatest temptation to tampering. One she set in the kitchen cabinet, one by the cereal and sugar, another on the steps leading to her room. In the hall she set three spaced six feet apart. Having insured the detection of anyone who roamed the house that night, she retired. She promised herself that she would sleep light as a feather, one eye would remain half open. She would hear the traps should they be snapped. With a heart primed with vengeance, she fell asleep. It is to be deplored that she could not break her neck falling to sleep.

During the day a clock tells the time without effort; at night it seems to labor at dragging the minutes by. When the Imp came down the hall he thought that only he and the clock were awake. Tick-iti-tock. Tick-iti-tock. He bore his hatpin lance, and, holding it over his head, he did a little jig in time with the tick-iti-tock, tick-iti-tock.

"I am being a soft-shoe dancer."

He stopped his dance when he spied the three traps strung along the hall. He leaned on his lance while he studied them.

"If it is being yesterday, maybe I am dashing up to see what these contraptions might be. But I am wising up with each injury. I am making haste slowly."

He approached the first trap and his nose began to dance for the morsel of cheese that Seppy had set in the snare. His nose began to pull him forward fast. He reached the trap, was about to step into it. His foot was raised when he heard a tiny squeak. He froze with his foot uplifted. He looked out of the corners of his eyes. Slowly, with the utmost quiet, he withdrew his foot. Crouching, he was poised for flight back to his cave should any monstrous thing leap out at him. He waited. Bringing up the hatpin, he set the big beaded head against his chest and held his lance in battle position.

The squeak came again, a piteous, small sound. The Imp jumped half an inch in fright and took two backward steps. All around him he peered. He gnashed his teeth. He prodded the air with his lance.

"If I am wearing shoes, I am thinking they are squeaking; but I am shoeless as caterpillars. Maybe there is a giant being at large; but if I am hearing his shoes squeaking, I should be hearing also his foot-steppings."

Three squeaks in close succession came to his ears.

"Whoever is squeaking these squeaks, is squeaking in the kitchen," he determined. With his lance couched for attack he edged along the wall toward the kitchen.

The trap that Septuagesima had set on the kitchen floor had snared a victim. It had caught a mouse. The mouse had snatched the cheese and almost gotten away. The bar of the trap, however, had clamped down on his tail. A sturdy fellow, sleek and gray, he had dragged the trap until it lodged and was caught against the leg of the table. He was held for fair, and all his panting and pulling were to no avail.

The Imp looked at the mouse. The mouse looked at the Imp.

"You are looking like a mouse."

The mouse was not ashamed. He squeaked again.

"You are sounding like a mouse."

The mouse looked imploringly at the Imp. His eyes told that it was not the time to be deciding that a mouse looks like a mouse and sounds not otherwise. Here he was with his handsome tail cut almost in half, and the Imp was telling him that he sounded like a mouse. His eyes spoke to the Imp:

"I am sorry that I have squeaked if you object to squeaking. At this moment I wish I were a lion, and I would roar like a lion. If you object to my squeaking, you will not have long to object, for I have little more than half a dozen squeaks left if this diabolical machine is not removed from my tail. In verity and verily the pain is killing me; and if the pain does not kill me, I will shortly bleed to death. I will be utterly sad to die, because there is so much of this and so much of that which is good in life, especially chestnuts."

To the mouse said the Imp: "I am not knowing whether it is safe to spring you from this trap. You are making times of me in weighing in, and I am having more enemies loose than a few."

The mouse's eyes declared: "I am without exception the meekest mouse in mousedom. I will serve you faithfully and well until the end of my days—if you will undo my tail and keep my days from ending today."

The Impulsive Imp pondered the matter while the mouse increased his panting to arouse sympathy in the Imp's breast. The Imp examined the tail and saw that it was cut almost in half. Recalling the agony of a blister on his own tail, he allowed his heart to be touched.

"You are being in a sorry state. This trap which is catching you is no doubting the work of my archenemy to be killing me. You are saving my life, in a way; so I will be saving yours."

The Imp set about freeing the mouse. Standing on the trap, he gripped the crossbar and strained until his face turned black with the effort. The mouse panted patiently.

"Shades and shanks!" swore the Imp. "This Seppy cook should be frying in her own grease."

The mouse assented with a doleful sigh.

The Imp next endeavored to insert his lance between the crossbar and the end of the trap; but the crossbar fitted over the edge of the wood. The spring was tight as a wisdom tooth. The point of the lance, slipping off the crossbar, caused the shaft to vibrate until the Imp's teeth chattered.

"This is being a situation demanding the tapping of untapped resources," the Imp told the mouse.

"Kind Imp, I am placing myself in your hands," the mouse implied. "Do with me what you will, for I am grown too weak to will. Almost too weak to squeak." He squeaked thinly to test how fast his strength was ebbing.

"We are facing an emergency. Mouse, are you submitting yourself to surgery?"

With both eyes the mouse submitted.

The Imp dashed down the hall, using his lance to pole-vault over the sills. As he scaled the chimney to his cave, he chanted:

"Calling Doctor Imp. Calling Doctor Imp!"

When he stood before the mouse again, the Imp was equipped with his razor blade and a piece of the thread he had purloined from Septuagesima's dresser top. The mouse's eyes were closed and his breathing was irregular.

"Hm-m-m," he hummed with his head cocked wisely, "My patient is Cheyne-Stoking. There is being no time for anesthesia even if I am having same. I could be bopping him on the head to be knocking him out; but that is also killing him, maybe."

He put his finger to an artery just above the rodent's right eye. "Pulse is being rapid but strong. He is surviving surgery under the talented hands of Dr. Imp." He spat liberally into the palm of his hand and scrubbed up. "Absolute sterile techniquing."

The Imp took a position behind the mouse. He braced himself with one foot against the trap. "If I am having soap, I am shaving the area of operations. But no soap, no prepping."

He raised the blade above his head, and fixed his eyes upon the site of amputation. Then he closed his eyes. The blade descended. Zip, and the tail was severed. Half a handsome tail remained in the trap. The Imp opened his eyes.

"Complimenting you, Dr. Imp. It is being a clean guillotine amputation." Dropping the blade he snatched up the thread. "Now to be tying off the stump."

The Imp gently wound the thread just short of the end of what remained of the mouse's tail. Finished, he stood back to view his work.

"I guess," he said, throwing out his chest, "I am the greatest Imp surgeon in the whole world."

CHAPTER 11

The mouse's head rested on his outstretched forelegs. His eyes were shut, and he breathed slowly and regularly. The Imp pushed back one of his eyelids.

"He is passing out cold as ice cream in December."

The Imp climbed up the drainpipe of the kitchen sink. From the border of the sink he pulled himself up to the hot-water faucet. Standing on the faucet he could reach the edge of a dishtowel that hung from a rack.

"With this," he said, "I will be covering my patient. I am no doubting he is suffering from shock, and he might be dying before he sees what a beauteous amputation I am doing on his tail."

He covered the mouse with the cloth. After cutting off a small patch with which to bandage the tail, he tucked in the cloth all around. "And now, I will be setting out to foil this Seppy cook whose heart is knowing kindness like I am knowing calculus."

The trap that had snapped on the mouse's tail served to teach the Imp how the gadgets worked. With his hands behind his back and a scowl on his face, he minutely examined the machine of torture. He climbed across the rectangular slot of wood and read the instructions printed upon it.

"This is being an ingenious contraption," he concluded. "They are making twenty turns for a spring. It is being strong enough, no doubting, to break all my legs. If ever I am growing beyond my vest-pocket size, I am building a trap like this—but big enough to be catching this Seppy cook, this marble-hearted, knuckle-headed Seppy cook. It is being most inhumane to inflict capital punishment on imps and mice because they are being guilty of hunger."

The Imp shouldered his lance and sought out the traps in the hall. Approaching each trap from the safe side, he hammered on the catch with the beaded end of the hatpin. After each trap had harmlessly snapped, he removed the bait. Bringing the three pieces of cheese to the kitchen, he set them down under the mouse's nose. The mouse remained unconscious.

"If cheese is not reviving my patient," he sighed, "I am hardly knowing what to do next—except to be eating the cheese."

Having eaten the cheese with gusty relish, he cut another piece from the dish cloth and climbed up to the sink again. One of the faucets was dripping with the rhythm of a beating heart. He put the cloth under the drip, and sat down to wait for it to be soaked.

"This is being too slow," he complained. "I am waiting here all night for this rag to get damp. He mounted to the faucet and tugged at the handle. Because it did not move, he kicked at it.

"I am breaking my ankle for this mouse." He rubbed the bruised joint. "But a doctor must be making sacrifices for his patient. It is being in keeping with the Hypocritical oath."

Water issued from the faucet in a thin but steady stream that soon saturated the cloth. The Imp threw the wet cloth to the floor and climbed down.

"It is being a wet compress," he informed the unconscious mouse as he placed the cloth across the mouse's forehead. "Now you will be opening your eyes in no time flat."

The water, flowing in a jagged stream across the sink, began to gabble down the drain.

The Imp grimaced. "This is being a most unpleasant hullabaloo. Like tom-cats and geese under the house."

Once again he climbed up to the sink. He found the rubber stopper and stamped it into place. Then he pulled himself out of the sink onto the drainboard. The water puddled up around the stopper. The puddle became a shallow pool that shortly covered the bottom of the sink.

"If it is being summer time," said the Imp, "I am giving myself a lesson in Australian crawling."

He lowered his toe to feel the water. He was prepared to pull back foot, and a br-r-r-r was ready on his lips. To his surprise, he found the water warm. The stream was coming from the hot-water faucet.

"Why I am never having it so good before! A private pool like the cinnamon stars. While my mouse is playing sleeping pretty, I will go Buster Crabbing."

He jerked his jacket over his head, and pulled off his pantaloons. His cap he hung on the handle of the faucet. With his lance he pried loose a partially used bar of floating soap, and sent it skidding down the drainboard into the water.

"To boot, I am having a diving raft," he exulted.

He took a position at the edge of the board and looked down into his exclusive pool. "Now, what am I doing for my first dive? A swoon dive or a pocketknife? Maybe I should be doing a half gainer or a triple twist. I am deploring the fact that there are being no spectators."

He rose gracefully to his toes. Where he stood, the soap had made a slippery spot. His feet flew from under him, and he hit the water in an exemplary *belly bust*. He disappeared through the middle of the splash. When he came to the surface he was churning the water like a steamboat paddle. The soap raft bobbed in front of him. He clung to it. Coughing and

"While you are guzzling that, I will be commandeering an ambulance to remove you. It is not being long before a deluge is hitting this vicinity."

The Imp spoke with assurance upon the matter of acquiring an ambulance. A patient should always be spoken to with assurance. He dashed out into the alcove as though he knew exactly where an ambulance was to be had. Once out of sight of the mouse, however, he stopped and scratched at the perplexity in his head.

"Necessity is being the mother of invention; and where there is being the will, there is being a way; but this is not bringing me an ambulance. It is being like a stitch in time saving nine when I am having no thread; and an ounce of prevention being worth a pound of cure when I am having no scale."

The door of the parents' room was open, but the Imp knew that in there slept the monster whose awakening had sent him zooming up the shade.

"I am not hankering for any thrills, chills and spills that come with playing tag with a window shade; but if I am not finding a convenient conveyance, my mouse patient is any minute floating out of the kitchen."

The Imp gnashed his teeth for courage. The life or death need of the mouse gave him resolution to overcome his trepidation. Into the father's room he slipped as quietly as a sigh. He searched the room without immediate reward. Balefully he looked upon the mother and the father.

"If I am having the strength, I am tumbling you two out on your elbow and putting my patient into this bed." To his ear came the sound of water cascading from the sink to the floor. The Imp hopped from one foot to the other with urgency. He tripped over the father's shoe. "Here is being the answer to my problem," he exulted. "I am being most thankful that virtue is being rewarded."

With alacrity he withdrew the lace of one shoe from all but the bottom gimlets. Pulling the ends of the lace out beyond the toe of the shoe he tied them together. Then he stepped inside the loop and raised it until the knot was against his chest.

"Be mushing you malamute," he growled as he threw his weight against the harness. His feet slipped on the floor, and for an interminable two seconds he ran frantically without advancing an inch. The lace across his chest saved his falling; and, regaining his balance, he pushed forward again. The shoe came sliding behind him.

"Come on," he cried to the mouse who had risen on wobbly legs, "climb in. Already you are having wet feet."

With the Imp's assistance, the mouse crawled across the toe of the shoe and down between the perforated flaps. His legs gave way, and he sank down upon the tongue. He lay troubled for breath while the Imp leaped again into harness. He threw his weight first to one side, then to the other, and then full force forward. The shoe moved a mite. Quickly he took a little slack and thrust forward again mightily. A zigzag vein swelled out on his forehead, and, for a moment, he was blinded by the blood that surged behind his eyes. He bore forward undaunted, and the shoe came after him steadily. With his arms stretched behind him and his hands burning along the lace, he strained on and on. His chin seemed to be digging a hole in his chest. Each step down the hall was a titanic accomplishment. Each breath was fire in his throat. The sprung traps in the hall were milestones on the seemingly endless road to the living room. Midway down the hall, he rolled his eyes upward to see how far he had yet to go.

"Before I am reaching the end," he gasped, "my heart is exploding into little pieces."

He advanced until his lungs seemed to come up into his mouth in search of air. His tongue hung out further and further. On and on he pulled the shoe: the length of the hall, across the living room, under the bookcase. At the end of his journey his knees buckled and he lay across the shoelace. All the air in the world seemed not enough to fill his lungs. All the weight in the world seemed not enough to keep his heart from jumping in his breast. Gradually, however, he came to breathe more easily, and his heart returned to its unobtrusive beating. He felt curiously rested despite his tremendous exertions.

"You are waiting here," he told the mouse, "until I am coming back again. Lie still and be sleeping. While the day is lighting the house, you should not be showing even the tip of your tongue. Enemies are surrounding us."

The mouse opened his eyes and nodded his head slightly.

"And now I am going up to my cave to be resting my aching bones." The Imp patted the mouse's head. "Good night."

The Imp was ankle deep in the ashes of the grate when he spun around. He was sure he had heard a voice say: "Good night." He looked at the shoe under the bookcase, for the "good night" seemed to have come from there. There came no further sound. When he retraced his steps to the shoe, he found his patient lying, eyes closed, snug between the flaps.

"He is breathing deep like sleepers. Maybehaps I am talking to myself."

Up in his cave, when sleep was pressing upon his eyes, a startling realization awakened him.

"If I am talking to myself and telling myself 'good night,' why am I using somebody else's voice?"

CHAPTER 13

The mother drifted on the nameless barge that plies between sleep and waking. Without a helmsman, the barge slipped first into the utter blackness of sleep, and then reappeared, as from a fog, to float through a dim light. Almost imperceptibly it fell in with a current that tugged tautly at it to give it direction and a destination. With steadily and stealthily increasing speed it made way. It hurried past vague, narrowing shores toward a distant murmuring. It sped toward a growing sound. It raced through an awful roaring. On the brink of a cataract that fell away to a frothy depth, it paused. Then, with the abruptness of a sea gull's diving, it plunged down. The mother thrashed the bed such as a drowning person beats the water. She delivered the father a hefty blow on the cheek.

"Wake up," he urged, shaking her. "Wake up! Are you trying to disfigure me?"

The mother opened her eyes to a room ghostly with the dawn's beginning.

"What has possessed you?" the father asked. "You're punching me in your dreams. What a nasty turn for the subconscious to take."

"I wasn't punching; I was swimming."

"It's the wrong time, and definitely the wrong place."

"It was a dream," she explained, "and I was going over something like Niagara Falls and swimming to save my life."

"When you're going over something like Niagara Falls, it's no use to swim."

"I was about to be dashed against the rocks when you woke me up. It's one dream I sure don't mind having interrupted. Thank you, dear."

"Think nothing of it," he said. "It was self-defense."

"It was a most vivid dream," she went on, "the river, the shores and the water falling way down. It seems to me I can still hear the water falling. The subconscious is a powerful thing."

The father yawned. The mother ignored it.

"I must remember to read a book that explains this dream."

She lay still for a moment waiting for him to reply, to agree on the power of the subconscious. He, however, had gone off again to sleep. She did not try to regain sleep, but lay listening intently to the echo of the water that had fallen in her dream. Never before, she thought, had she had a dream that had lingered on so. After a while, she decided to get up and drip some coffee. She put her foot to the floor but withdrew it quickly. The father started up when she jabbed him in the ribs.

"What, in heaven's name, are you dreaming now?" he asked.

"There is something very strange about this dream," the mother informed him. "When I put my foot to the floor, you know it felt just like water."

"Why do you wake me up with this nonsense?" the father grumbled. "You're as bad as Alice. There's only about sixty winks left to this night, and you're going to steal them."

The mother was feeling her toes. "There is water on the floor," she said. "Do you realize there's water on the floor?"

"Let me feel your toes." The father wiped his fingers on the sheet. "Just a little dampness. Let's go back to sleep. It might have come from anywhere."

"Maybe there's a flood. Maybe a river has overflowed."

"We don't live by any river," he said. "Probably a little snow that blew in through the window."

"The rug would have absorbed a little snow. I do wish you'd get up and put on the light."

"In a little while there will be enough daylight to see by. Why don't you forget the dream and get a little more sleep?"

"It isn't only a dream" she objected. "I can still hear water falling."

"The sound of water falling should put you to sleep."

"But the floor's wet," she exclaimed, exasperated.

"You don't have to sleep on the floor. Why worry about it?"

"I will worry about my floor. And if you love me, you'll get up and turn on the light."

The father surrendered. Kicking back the blankets, he put his feet to the floor. "Wow!" he exclaimed, pulling his feet onto the bed. "It's icy cold!"

"You see. I told you so."

The father hugged his knees and shivered. "You think a pipe's broken somewhere?"

"It sounds like a faucet's been running all night."

"Confound it! What's going to happen next in this house?"

"Slip on your shoes and turn on the light."

Of course, he could find only one shoe. He groped under the bed, splashing water and muttering imprecations.

"Are you ever going to turn on the light?" she asked.

"I can't find my other shoe," he almost shouted.

"What did you do with it?"

"I put it under the bed where I always put it."

"Maybe it floated away," the mother suggested.

"The water isn't that deep—thank goodness."

With a "whoo-hoo" he ran bare-footed to the wall and snapped on the light. The floor of the bedroom was thin sheeted with water.

"Goodness gracious!" the mother cried, "everything will be ruined."

"The bed's still dry," the father commented as he leaped into it.

"This is no time for levity," declared the mother. She had put on her shoes, and was digging in the closet for her galoshes.

"Time, really, for levitation," he muttered. He sat in the middle of the bed, drying his feet on the blanket. "If you'll throw me my other shoes, I'll breast this flood and see how the kitchen stands—if it still does."

The alcove floor and the kitchen floor were inundated, and long fingers of water were reaching down the hall.

The father turned off the running faucet, and turned on the gas heater in the kitchen. Wearing overcoats, he and the mother began sweeping the water out of the kitchen door. Septuagesima, hearing their noise, came down from her room.

"What are you doing?" she inquired.

"Just keeping busy, Seppy," the Father snarled. "Just keeping busy."

"We woke up and found the place flooded," the mother informed the cook.

"How'd it happen?"

"The faucet over the sink was left running last night," said the mother. "Could you get a mop and come after us?"

"There ought to be a union," Seppy mumbled, but she lighted the oven of the stove to further counteract the cold wind rushing in through the open door. She picked up the dishcloth that the Imp had used to cover his patient, and draped it on the sink. When she mopped under the kitchen cabinet, she pulled out the trap that still held the mouse's tail. She failed to notice the tail, however, until after she had picked up the trap. With a frightened squeal she dropped the trap, and rubbed her hands against her dress.

"What's the matter?" the mother asked.

"There's a tail in the trap." Seppy shuddered at the thought of fleas.

"Whose tail?" asked the father.

"A rat's tail."

The mother examined the trap. "I think it must be a mouse tail. The trap is hardly large enough to cut off a rat's tail. But it does seem to be a pretty long one. "Will you take it out, dear," she said to the father, "and put it in the garbage can?"

"Don't you think we should bury it with some sort of ceremony?"

"Please—" said the mother, "it might have fleas or lice on it."

The father picked up the trap. "Just think: somewhere a little mouse is probably bleeding to death."

"This is no time for morbid sympathy for mice," said the mother.

"Still," the father insisted, "a trap is unsportsmanlike. If we're after mice for stealing the cookies and nibbling holes in the cereal boxes, I think we ought to let the cat stay in at night. It won't just bite off some poor mouse's tail."

Alice appeared in the kitchen doorway.

"The hall is just full of mice traps," she spread the news, "but not any mice."

"You get back to bed, young lady," the father ordered, "or I'll get down my cat-o-nine-tails."

"Where'd all the water come from?" asked Alice. "Where's a cat with nine tails?"

The father bowed to the mother. "I wash my hands of the whole affair—and that isn't hard to do with the amount of water available in these parts. I'll take this mouseless tail and build myself an igloo in the back yard."

"Alice," the mother took over, "run back immediately and get into bed."

"You always want me to be in bed," claimed Alice. "You think I want to stay in bed all the time"

"Back to bed, please. We have work to do."

"You think I don't know how to work," charged Alice.

"Back to bed."

"I hate bed," Alice stated as she retreated down the hall.

CHAPTER 14

Septuagesima made a pot of coffee. The mother and father, after their labor, sat down thankfully to the hot brew. The father luxuriously relished the flow of warmth through his throat right down to his stomach. He took a swallow and waited with a beatific expression for the warmth to run through him.

Septuagesima looked at him with disdain and disgust for expressing so obviously a purely sensuous pleasure.

"You know," he said, "hot coffee on a cold morning is a sensual thing."

Septuagesima started as though he had read her thoughts. The mother was preoccupied.

"Despite the ads in the summer time," the father continued, "coffee is not particularly tasty. It's the warmth that counts. Warmth is one with coffee. Coffee without hotness is like a postman without mail. Heat milk or lemonade, and you have medicine. Tea probably tastes better cold than hot. Hot water is good only for a bath or a hot-water bottle. But hot coffee! There you have romance and adventure. I can drink hot coffee at 4 in the morning, and feel like a world-weary, sin-wise newspaper reporter. I can feel the steely spearhead of rain, and hear the winds gone wild as I stand on the bridge of my ship and scream against the gale for a mug of piping hot Java. I can see myself hunched over the counter of a little roadside inn, drinking a cup of Joe, relaxing my muscles, while my interstate van stands outside, its engine rhythmically growling, primed for the next long haul; and I can see myself—."

"Look," said the mother, unkindly breaking the father's monologue, "I hate to be the one to introduce the awkward question, but who left the faucet running last night?"

"Gee whiz, did you have to do that?" asked the father.

Septuagesima, who had been seeing the father in a straitjacket while he saw himself as reporter, sea captain and truck driver, gave a snort to indicate that it was time somebody stopped him.

"I'm worried," said the mother, "very worried. There are too many unexplained things happening in this house."

"I agree with you, Ma'am," said Septuagesima.

"Let me make haste to agree with you too, Ma'am," said the father, "lest I become suspect."

"It isn't strange that a faucet was left running," the mother went on, "but it is strange that the stopper was left in. There was two-thirds of a dishcloth on the floor. What happened to the other piece?"

"And four of the traps I set last night were snapped," Seppy put in, "and we caught only a mouse's tail."

"Yes, and don't forget the cookies and the cereal," said the mother.

Seppy was about to mention what had happened in her room the night before, but she thought better of it.

"Tomorrow, when you're cleaning the house, please look for my shoe," the father told Seppy. "The only pair I've ever had that didn't hate my feet, and now one is missing."

"We're all talking," said the mother, "and nothing's getting explained. Who turned on the faucet last night?"

"That's a good question," said the father. "Another just as good is, who tore up the dish cloth?"

"And who snapped the traps?" was Seppy's question.

"Perhaps the mouse who lost only his tail snapped the traps," the father suggested.

"Could a mouse tear a dish cloth in half?" asked Seppy.

"They're pretty smart critters."

"Grant a mouse snapped the traps and tore the cloth," said the mother, "would you say a mouse turned on the faucet and put in the stopper?"

"I wouldn't go so far as to say that," the father hedged, "but let the mouse account for the traps and dish cloth, and then let's say that Septuagesima, perhaps, left the faucet running."

"We won't say anything of the sort," Seppy defended herself. "I didn't leave the faucet running. I was the last to go to bed because I stayed up to set the traps; but I did not leave the faucet on."

"Well then" said the father, "I ask no one in particular; but, who turned on the faucet?"

"Maybe whoever took your shoe turned on the faucet," snapped Seppy, "and I have no use for your shoe."

The mother pondered. "I wonder if Alan could have come back here during the night. He has a sail boat."

"Perhaps he sailed my shoe," said the father. "He could have used the dish cloth for a sail."

Septuagesima did not believe that Alan had done anything of the sort. She felt a strengthening conviction that the father had walked away from his wits. No doubt he was maliciously crazy, and was trying to drive her into the same boat. She was reluctant to divert her suspicions away from the children. It had been more satisfactory to find them and their father in cahoots.

When they sat before the fire that evening, Alan confided to Alice.

"I think I'm going to run away from home. Everything that happens around here I get blamed for."

"Me too," said Alice.

"They think I put daddy's shoe in the sink last night."

"I don't think you did."

"I haven't even seen his shoe." Alan's sorrow for himself increased under Alice's sympathy. "I don't even know what color it is. I don't even know if it was the left or the right shoe."

"Me neither," said Alice.

"When a boy has to go to school," said Alan, reaching the depth of depression, "he's got enough trouble. He shouldn't have any trouble at home."

CHAPTER 15

The Imp came out of a deep sleep and went into a brown study.

"Now that I am slept out, I will be giving some little thought to the voice I am hearing last night. It is bad hearing voices if there is being no voices; worse than not hearing voices when there are voices."

He meditatively scratched some soot from his scalp.

"I am wondering about that mouse I am operating on last night. Maybehaps, he is being a spying mouse, trained by my enemies to be decoying me. If that is being a fact, I will be operating on his neck."

The Imp wet his finger on his tongue, dipped it in some soot and began to clean his teeth. Absentmindedly he rubbed his finger back and forth.

"If this is being an informing mouse, why is he catching his tail in the trap?"

Catching only his tail might be part of the plan of deception. Being placed at the Imp's mercy, he might more easily gain the Imp's confidence.

"But my enemies are not knowing about me," the Imp assured himself. "I am going about quiet like snakes in wet grass—except when misfortunes are burning my tail and running me up shades. My mouse patient is being, no doubt, a legitimate mouse."

The Imp finished cleaning his teeth and tidied up his cave. He shoved the soot over the edge, watched it shower into the grate, and shortly followed it down. He cocked both ears for sounds. There were no sounds. He sniffed for danger. There was no danger to be sniffed.

The mouse was sitting in the shoe preening his whiskers. The Imp climbed up on the toe of the shoe and sat down.

"Hello, mouse."

For a moment the mouse hesitated. He studied the Imp, gauging the character of his savior.

"Hello," he then ventured, his voice soft like low music.

The Imp, to say a little less than least, was taken aback. With one motion he rose to his feet and took up his tail.

"So I am being right. I am hearing you say 'hello'; and when I am leaving you, I am hearing you say 'good night.'"

"It is true as blue that I wished you good night," said the mouse, "and I trust you had a sleep that was this and that and most restful."

"You are giving me bad dreams with your wishing when I'm not knowing you are speaking anything but squeaking."

"It regrets me this way and that and much that I repaid with bad dreams all your trouble on my behalf."

"It is not mattering." The Imp sat down again. "But when I am finding you with your tail in the trap, why are you not talking to me then?"

"I was afraid I might frighten you away. Mice are not ordinarily built for speech. And I needed you dearly and direly."

"And you are being an honest mouse? You are not coming from my enemies to be infiltrating me?"

"I am more honest than the mirror on the wall. I am a stranger and stranded in these parts. Your enemies are my enemies; your friends, my friends."

"I am having no friends."

The mouse stood up. "If you will pardon my saying so and such, and will not think me brash and bold, I am offering myself to you as a warm and willing friend."

The Impulsive Imp was touched deeply. Bashfully, he wound his tail around his hand. Embarrassed, he dropped his tail and rubbed his palms along the legs of his pantaloons. "I am being glad to have a friend."

The mouse kissed the Imp on the cheek, further embarrassing him and tickling him no little.

"No doubting, you are hungry," said the Imp, stepping back and almost falling from the toe of the shoe. "If you are waiting here no time at all, I am getting you something to eat."

The Imp, desiring to do some nice thing for his first friend, was about to dash off to the kitchen. He had in mind the cereal boxes stacked on the shelf. The mouse restrained him.

"I am no inconsequential mouse in the part where my parts are known. I am an eloquent mouse always, and, on occasion, even grandiloquent. I am a leader of and pleader for my tribe. Since you have saved an important life, I will render you and lend to you my services. I am hereafter and henceforward your mount."

Such a magnanimous offer astounded the Imp and humbled him. He pretended that he did not understand.

"What needing have I for a mount? I am going to the top of the chimney and having all the mounts I am needing. This vicinity is abounding in mounts: snow covered, large, small and all around."

"You deliberately misconstrue my offer." The mouse further swallowed his pride. "I do not mean mounts such as Pikes Peak and Lookout. I speak of mount such as a nag, a stallion, or this or that kind of quadruped that lends itself to the service of a rider."

"You mean," said the Imp, "that I should be riding on your back?"

"Exactly and explicitly."

The Imp regarded the mouse. The idea of having a mount set his imagination to running. He saw himself decked out in the habiliments of Mars and riding off to war.

"How glorious it is being. But I cannot be doing this. You are my friend."

"No friend is caviling or questioning the service of a friend."

The Imp still hesitated.

"Climb on my back," the mouse ordered, "and we will go here and there, hither and thither that you might learn the nature of my stride."

With the Imp on his back, the mouse set out at a trot. He circled the room. He passed beneath the chairs, and the Imp felt his cap brush against the rungs. He held his seat by holding on to the mouse's ears.

"Now we will try a run." And the mouse increased speed until the Imp felt the breath catch in his throat. He was flying. Three times around the room the mouse sped, and then came to a skidding halt. The Imp slid forward to the mouse's neck.

"And now I will gallop, and go this way and that to see if you can stick should we ever have to flee and fly before an enemy."

The next moment the Imp was holding on for life. The mouse darted about the room, first to the right, then to the left. He slowed for a moment, and then sprang forward like a streak. The Imp swayed from side to side, shouted yee-ee and hoo-o-o, fell forward and was jerked back. Finally, the mouse leaped to the seat of Alice's rocking chair. He slid two inches, dug in and stopped with back humped like a bronco's.

"You are an equestrian," the mouse complimented the Imp. "You are also being a great rider."

The Imp dismounted. Something new had entered his life, an experience that made a foundation upon which his ego could stand. He felt no longer the need to tell himself that he was the greatest this and the greatest that in the whole wide world. Of one thing he had become sure. He was the most expert mouse rider that ever lived.

"I am being a knight, that's what I'm being," he exulted. "I am dubbing myself Sir Imp. And you are being the most magnificent mount a knight is ever having."

The mouse dropped him a curtsy. "Indeed you are Sir Imp, a knight of the night. I can tell at a glance the smite of your lance will fill tomes of romance. And now Sir Imp, whither away and where shall we be off to?"

"You will be resting here," the Imp commanded. "You are panting from the racing. I will be getting us something to be eating."

The Imp sped down the hall on feet swift with joy. His head was a cauldron boiling with ideas. If he could round up some more imps and mount them on mice, he would organize the knights of the square table. He would watch over and defend the princess with the spun golden hair, the princess that slept in the old-fashioned bed. Contrary to his custom of alertness, he was half in a dream while he climbed up the handle of the refrigerator and thence to the shelf where the boxes of cereal were stacked. Standing behind one of the boxes, he pushed. The box hit the top of the refrigerator and bounced, end over end, to the floor.

Drip, the cat, who lay under the kitchen cabinet, opened his eyes and blinked them like slow shutters. He eyed the box, and decided that, in a world where so obnoxious a thing as rain fell, a box of cereal falling to the floor was of little moment. He went back to sleep. The Imp, unaware of Drip as Drip was unaware of him, shouldered the small box and went quietly down the hall.

CHAPTER 16

The Imp unshouldered the box at the mouse's feet.
"It is being a cereal," he said, "which I am hoping will continue for a long time. Pardon my punning, but are you being hungry?"

"As wolves and wind, and in all ways and famished," the mouse replied.

"Then be guarding this booty while I am going to get my sword to be slashing it up and down."

"There is no need. I will gnaw our way into this container."

"You will be doing nothing of the sort. I am needing the practice with my sword."

The Imp returned from the cave, and with three accurate, vicious slashes lay open the side of the box. He and the mouse sat down to the heap of pellets that flooded out. They fell to with gusto.

"This is delectable, delicious and most probably nutritious," said the mouse. "With all these vitamins, I will, without question, be able to bear you far and enduringly."

"I am sorry I am not finding you some cheese," said the Imp.

"Do not concentrate on it nor be concerned. I do not especially care for cheese."

"You are being a mouse and not liking cheese?"

"I am not an ordinary mouse. And I think that, particularly since you have shown no inquisitiveness, it is right and just that I tell you who I am and wherefore I am here."

"Not at all," the Imp protested. "You are already proving yourself to me. I am not inquiring into your past."

"Before this delicious repast is past, and I trust it will not be our last, I will have told you all about myself," the mouse insisted. "To do so is a debt, I feel, that I owe you for having saved my life and some small amount of my tail."

There ensued a moment of sympathetic silence during which the Imp avoided looking at the mouse's loss of nobility. The mouse gulped in sharp sorrow over his ignoble loss.

"It's of no moment and no matter," he bravely continued. "When I was born my father called me Roddy Phenocomps Longicauda. I am known in my family as Roddy, and you will please me much and more if you will henceforward address me so."

"I am being proud to do so," said the Imp warmly. "I am being glad, indeed, to be knowing you, Roddy."

"Thank you. Well, I grew fast in the fresh air and sunshine of the tip-top of our pine tree. I developed a beautiful singing voice, and learned to speak with eloquence."

"You are proving that," said the Imp. "I am loving to hear you sing."

"With pleasure," said Roddy. "Later."

They halted their conversation to make another attack on the dwindling pile of pellets. The sound of crunching and crackling was like soft laughter in the living room.

"Two months ago," Roddy picked up his tale, "word came to our tribe that all the rodent tribes in this country's continental limits were to send representatives to a Grand Council that was to be presided over by the Rattus norvegicus. The P. longicauda are an exclusive and seclusive tribe. We preferred having naught and nothing to do with this Council. However, we dared not refuse, because the word had come from the Chief of the Norvegicus. It is a most fearsome tribe."

"If you are pardoning my saying so," interjected the Imp, "this is being a long story." With his taste for trouble and near disaster, the Imp strained his patience to sit still out of harm's way.

"It is longer," said Roddy calmly. "But there is no cause for huff and haste. The supply of cereal is copious and our stomachs are capacious. Since I was the most eloquent member of our tribe, I was chosen to represent the Phenocomps longicauda at the Council."

"Your tribe is being wise in honoring you." The Imp nodded his head gravely and stuffed his mouth with pellets.

"Yes, I felt honored; but no less I felt a large fearfulness, because no member of the Rattus norvegicus is to be honored or esteemed."

"I am hating these Norvegicans already." The Imp gnashed his teeth.

"I quit the glint and glory of our tree top and set out," Roddy continued. "When I put up the first dawn at Asotin, Washington, intending that night to find some means of crossing the Snake River, I met Red. I was seeking a tree wherein and in which to build a temporary nest, and I found him huddled at the base of a pine tree—and he was pining no little."

"Why are you calling him Red?" asked the Imp. "Is he being a mouse also?"

"I called him Red because the hair along his back was red. He was a mouse; but, alas and alack, he is no longer. The Chief of the Norvegicus had him liquidated. He was drowned in a sewer."

"What is he doing in a sewer?" the Imp inquired.

"I have run and raced ahead of my story," said Roddy. "When I met Red I spoke to him, saying somewhat as follows:

'Why do you shiver and quiver like an aspen leaf? You are a handsome Red Mouse who should have no rhyme or reason for hiding and huddling out of sight among the roots of a tree.' He replied with much fluttering and stuttering, which, for the sake of brevity, I will omit. He told me he had been elected to represent his tribe, the Clethrionomys, at the Grand Council."

"Was he, too, being afraid of the Norvegicans?" asked the Imp.

"His was a mortal terror, my noble friend. Three weeks before he was chosen to represent his tribe, he had seen his mother slain and slaughtered by two Brown Rats."

"This is being a sad story," said the Imp, losing some of his appetite for the golden pile before him.

"Doleful and dolorous," Roddy shook his head. "Before I have reached the end and am done, you will weep until you have no more tears to weep. I comforted Red and smuggled him across the river. Together he and I crossed the continent: ferried rivers, climbed mountains, sleeping by day, traveling by night. On our way, we met a field mouse, a deer mouse and a kangaroo mouse making haste to the Council.

"In Michigan we encamped one day in a ripped and rusted boiler in a lovely junk-yard. It came that time of the evening when the sun seemed set for rolling around the rim of the world. We were sharing a loaf of stale bread, something to stand by us during the trek and traipse through the night. Suddenly, standing over us like the very approach of night, was a black Rattus rattus. He was, for a moment, silent and solemn. In courageous phalanx, we faced him. We thought surely he intended to purvey and purloin our supper. He rolled his eyes ingratiatingly, however, and addressed us somewhat to wit: 'Do not be afraid, little fellows. You have been called to a Council. Do not go; do not be duped! Turn back to your tribes.'

"We answered him that we had come too far to turn back, that our tribes would cast us out for cowardice. We knew, moreover and besides, that he might be talking just from bitterness because his tribe had suffered much from the teeth of the Rattus norvegicus. He looked at us, futility in the droop of his tail, and spoke somewhat accordingly: 'Look at me!' (We had no intent or intention of looking anywhere else.) 'I am a member of a lost tribe. I might shortly be an archaeological specimen. Time was when the world was ours. We were so populous in Egypt that our enemy, the cat, was made a deity. All Europe was ours: Germany, France, Spain and so forth. Africa was ours. We had Russia, Greece, Persia and the smaller countries around the Mediterranean. We became peace loving and averse to emigration. Short trips by sea made us seasick. We developed squeamish stomachs, and a squeamish stomach is tantamount to utter deterioration.'"

"This Black Rat is having also a silver tongue," commented the Imp.

"I am ghosting for him liberally if not too literally," said Roddy. "He speaks to us further much as follows: 'The news did not reach us until too late that the branch of our tribe in Persia had been exterminated by the vicious minority that suddenly grew to wicked proportions. This minority, as you probably have guessed, had been an insignificant tribe of Brown Rats. In less time than it takes to build a pyramid, the Brown Rats ruled Persia, India and China. Then came a memorable, misbegotten year of famine in China and India. There was no grain, no rice, not even leaves of trees. There were no chickens, no ducks, not even carcasses of cows and horses to satisfy the omnivorous appetite of the Brown tribe. Earthquakes shook Persia like an angry mother. The Brown Rats migrated in all directions. We tolerated the intruder. There was food enough for all; but the Brown Rat refused to share. He wanted all. He loved war, attacked us at every turn. Too long we had been accustomed to reign. We had grown fat, lazy and stupid. We who had seen thrones and dominations of men fall through the same defects, permitted ourselves to grow heavy with luxury and lethargic with ease.

"'We underestimated the strength of the Brown Rat. In Russia we mustered an army of twenty million and met the Brown on the field of the Ukraine. But we lacked leaders, and the enemy, individually, was the stronger. Though we outnumbered him, the Brown annihilated the Black. O the blood that flowed, the blood of my tribe, in a cataract of defeat. With one battle the Brown Rat had won all Russia, the Balkans, Austria and South Prussia.

"'My tribe lacked the will to fight. The Brown Rat seemed to come from everywhere at once. He swooped down from an Indian merchantman on England. The Black Rat, once the acme of nobility, went into hiding, paralyzed with fear, waiting meekly for destruction. And destruction came swiftly with long sharp teeth.

"'Yes, we made a stand in Paris. We lined the great sewers and fought to the death. Inglorious defeat, since so few remain to tell the valor manifest there. The corpses of our bravest warriors so congested the sewers that the beautiful filth and muck overflowed into the streets of Paris. The sewers of Paris! What a loss! What caverns, domes, palaces! Ask any Black Rat, of the few remaining, the year of his mightiest loss. He will tell you, 1754.

"'Everywhere we tried to surrender. We promised the Brown Rat we would eat nothing but grass. He derided the weakness of our capitulation. Ruthlessly he hunted us; heartlessly he slew us. He took Denmark, Switzerland, Sweden. He left us not even the cold countries.

"'From England the Brown Rat came to America. For a hundred years we fought him bitterly up and down the eastern coast, holding him east of the Appalachians. We sent word across the mountains, warning our brothers to prepare. Our incessant wars, however, drew so many millions from the other side, that, when the Brown Rat crossed the mountains in 1840, he marched straight through us to the Pacific Ocean. That was our end. A few thousands of us, who had once been hundreds of millions, live on an island off the coast of Maine; and our days are numbered.'

"The Black Rat paused for breath after this long and laborious chronicle," said Roddy. "We offered him a nibble of our bread. I could quibble about the size of his nibble. Then he groomed his whiskers wearily and told us he had gotten word of the Council. He decided upon a mission in life, to harangue against the Rattus norvegicus. He looked at each of us earnestly and spoke somewhat thus: 'The Brown Rat is a pillaging, perfidious, gluttonous, cunning, cruel, bloodthirsty rat, incapable of justice, mercy——.' He was about to enumerate further the incapabilities of the Brown Rat, when into the boiler leaped two gargantuan Norvegicans. The Black Rat curled his lips in a battle snarl and backed to the side of the boiler. The Brown Rats advanced on him, informing him that they had tracked him from the coast of Maine, that he was a malcontent and disperser of lies, that any rodent that spoke critically of the Norvegicans was worthy of death and worse. Though the Black Rat fought valiantly, the Browns treated him to death—and worse. When they had finished off the Black Rat, they turned to us; and, while finishing off our loaf of bread, told us to believe no word we had heard, but to proceed with haste to the Council. We did not stay to argue about the bread. We hit and hugged the road."

"I am not knowing I can sit still so long," breathed the Imp. "Let us be having another little snack, and you can be telling me some more."

CHAPTER 17

Roddy the rodent brushed away the golden flecks of cereal that had fallen onto the hairs of his chest.

"The Council," scoffed he, "is a caricature and a canard. We approach the city. The shining dome of the Capitol is suspended from the sky like a sea nettle in water. Though we are not going fast or furious, Red begins to pant unduly. We pause in the tall grass alongside the road. Nats, the Pocket Mouse, and Dippy, the Kangaroo Mouse, join with me in assuring and reassuring Red that there is nothing to fear or fret about. Because we are no little fearsome ourselves, our words do not ring sound and true, but Red comes on with us and does not die of fear on the spot.

"The night is not far enough gone for people to quit the night clubs and go home to bed. We have instructions to enter the main sewer through the lead-in on 12th Street, just off Pennsylvania Avenue. Though we are small and can glide along the curb, we do not care to run the risk of being stomped on. We stop, therefore, and wait by the Lincoln Memorial.

"I care little and less for men and the works of men, but I am glad we rest by this memorial. I know about this Lincoln Memorial since I am a baby. My father, no few times, uses the expression, when severe frost hits the conifers on our trees, that it is like looking for something to eat in the Lincoln Memorial. Not that he ever visits there; but he hears of a family of mice who put up there on the way West. They all starve to death. It is a marvel and marvelous to find a place frequented by people where there is not even a little bit of popcorn or peanuts, or the drippings and droppings from sandwiches. So I am glad to see this Lincoln Memorial."

"Someday I will be going there myself," said the Imp. "I'll be dignified and sitting on Lincoln's lap. When you are there, are you admiring Lincoln?"

"All I see," said Roddy, "is that he himself must have been short of rations. Well, the night gets old and crickety. We reach 12th Street without hap or mishap, and slide into the sewer. A Brown Rat is waiting for us. He pulls out a tape and measures our waist. He says he is finding out how many can fit into the Council chamber, but he is a lank fellow with a lusty look in his eye that makes us feel like pie. Nats and Dippy are carrying a bit of lunch in their cheek bags. He says to cough up, and slaps them on the back. Coughing up, they almost strangle. He asks Red what he means by being so small, and I tell him it is not Red's fault he is small. 'If all hairs are the same length, horses won't have tails.' He slaps me in the face, tells me I am a smart mouse with no right be alive. I wonder if I am having the right much longer.

"We go shoot-the-shooting down the pipe, the Brown Rat in front of us shouting instructions to turn left when we hit the water. For some time we swim along, working hard to keep up with the Brown Rat. He swims at a speed that won't lose us, but so fast that we half kill ourselves to keep him in sight.

"I do my best to see everything so that I will have markers in my mind. The water isn't deep enough and isn't running fast enough to float away all the debris. There are tin cans, a dead cat and part of a sign that reads: Open for Business.

"We arrive at a big circular chamber. It is wide at the bottom and narrows toward the top. I look up and see small circles of light like still stars. I know it is light sifting through the perforations in a manhole cover. Rung around this inverted funnel chamber are three shelves in tiers. Our guide tells us our places are on the top shelf. We scramble up the side. I do not have any trouble because I am a climber by nature, but Red is not used to climbing, not used to water. He is a good part numb with cold and fear. But there is much assistance. The shelves are packed with representatives from every rodent tribe in the country. They help us up.

"We squeeze into place on the third shelf. Red nudges me and asks what now. The Brown Rat shouts and says: 'Shut up now.' He has an acute ear.

"The chamber is quiet except for the dripping of water from the fur of the shivering assembly. At intervals the manhole cover rattles as an automobile drives across. After a while Red is less cold, for the bodies pressed against him give and communicate a warmth. The whole place is steaming.

"In the center of the chamber is a gallon-sized tin can with an oval shaped top. The can is anchored in mud, and the water flows slowly and thickly around it. Thirteen Brown Rats, in echelon, swim up to the can. The Chief of the Browns, large and arrogant, climbs up on the can. The other twelve divide into four parties of three each, and swim to the openings of the four conduits running from the chamber. There is no doubt or question that we are prisoners at the Council.

"The Chief looks up; and it seems that he looks at each one of us especially and particularly. 'Comrades,' he says, and pauses to let the salutation fill the chamber with its scorn. Red grunts a little. I am afraid he is about to object to being called 'comrade.' Anger is beginning to displace his fear. The Chief of the Norvegicans continues somewhat as follows:

"'I will not sashay around the bush. I am the leader of the Rattus norvegicus. I called you here for a purpose. The Rattus norvegicus rules this country. Every other country in the world also. I have it on good report that we hold Mars, too. We rule by right—and by night, ha, ha. The right of force. The right of strength. The right of the fittest and the fightenist.

"'As leader of the Norvegicus I am about to launch a vast program, a five-month plan. Each of your tribes has its place in this program. You are not Norvegicans. For that you are to be pitied, but no less despised.' (I hear Red almost strangling as he swallows this insult.)

"'Since food has become more expensive in this country,' the Chief of the Browns continues, 'people are not throwing as much away as they used to. Farmers are poisoning us in the wheat fields, the corn fields, in the vineyards. In warehouses electrical traps are being set up. We are finding some difficulty in satisfying our appetites.' (He eyed us, licking his thin lips, seeing a feast set before him.) 'We cannot spend all our time looking for something to eat. We must see to it that some few diseases are properly spread abroad in spite of the obstacles two-legged dunderheads are confronting us with: vaccination, sanitation, disinfectants, inoculations and a miscellany of truck and nonsense. We must see to it that great numbers of women are scared out of their wits. We must carry on the war against man: bore into drain pipes, gnaw away insulation on wires, set fires, dig through dams and undermine buildings.

"'You will comprehend our need when I tell you I am calling for ten thousand members from each of your tribes. You can inform your elders that it will be an honorable service. Each Rattus norvegicus must have a taster from another tribe to test for poison. Then there must be a reasonable reserve to replace the tasters who taste poison. Is there better reason to die than to lay down one's life to save that of a Norvegican!'

"The chamber is silent for a moment or such. The nerves of the representatives can almost be heard going taut and tense. I glance at Red. He is no longer shivering and shaking. I can see half his teeth as his lips draw back in scorn. The Brown Rats at the exits are searching the tiers for signs of dissent and dissatisfaction.

"The Chief of the Norvegicans hangs by his hind feet and takes himself a drink of water. He wipes his whiskers and faces us again.

"'I have one other thing to tell you,' he says, 'before we take a vote. What I am about to demand may, for the moment, repel you. However, I ask you to remember man, our host, with his concentration camps, incinerators and atomic bombs; and you will be more tolerant of the idea. The Norvegicans in foreign countries are faced with actual famine. The Brown Rat must not lose a toehold anywhere. Envision an earth over-run with men. From your tribes you will select the old, the unfit, the weak, the incompetents who can't tell cheese from crackers. I expect five thousand of these from each tribe. You will send them to the Atlantic and Pacific coastal towns where Brown Rats will round them up and smuggle them aboard ships bound for foreign countries and famished Norvegicans. Need I say more?'

"The rats guarding the exits beat the water in applause.

"'All of you in favor of these proposals,' went on the Chief, 'express it by a loud affirmative squeaking.'

"For a moment again the chamber is silent. The Brown Rats at the openings begin to move forward into the chamber. Behind them, as far as can be seen down the pipes, are streams of Norvegicans. There is a cacophony of affirmative squeaking. To my shame I must confess that I, too, squeak quite loudly.

"It is then that Red becomes a hero. He screams that never, never will his tribe be slaves of the Norvegicans or make one single sacrifice for the Browns. Blind with fury, he leaps for the throat of the Chief. But even his fury cannot carry him. His leap is short; and, with a cry in his throat, he falls into the water. The Brown Rats, churning from the exits, are instantly upon him. Before the eye can blink, the chamber swarms with Brown Rats. Red never rises from their snarling, tearing, boiling midst.

"The Chief calls for quiet and order. He asks if any other representative wishes to register an objection. Trapped in that death chamber, what can we do but consent? The Chief dismisses us, telling us to hasten back to our tribes with his instructions. He gives us thirty days to put his orders into effect.

"The Brown Rats have their sport with us, dunking and buffeting us as we swim down the pipes to the outlets."

"These Brown Rats," growled the Imp, "are being in the same classroom with Seppy cook."

CHAPTER 18

Roddy the rodent and the Impulsive Imp shared the last of the cereal, three pellets each. The Imp crushed a pellet meditatively.

"What will you be doing now?" he asked.

"I am on my way back to my tribe to tell them the demands of the Rattus norvegicus. I was passing this way, and this house had the seeming of a nice place to rest a little and a bit. I had been hastening and hurrying for forty-eight hours without water and victuals, for I must stop off and warn Red's tribe that the Brown Rats are up tooth and claw against them. I am not commonly or ordinarily fond of cheese, but my long fast made it inviting. I fell into the snare, was entrapped, detained and detailed."

"You must not be lingering here," said the Imp. "I am getting together some food to be taking with us. We will be leaving tonight." The Imp was urgent. "I will be going with you because I am a great warrior."

Roddy shook his head. He thanked the Imp in the name of his whole tribe for such a courageous offer. Were there twice ten million imps mounted on Phenocomps longicauda, then, possibly, a great battle might be fought. The Brown Rat might be eradicated from the land. But, alas, there was only one imp.

"I will stop and stay tonight," conceded Roddy, "that I might travel twice as fast tomorrow. But you must stay here. The rivers are too wide, the nights in the treetops too cold, the many and myriad of stinging insects in the field too much for you to endure."

The Imp was chagrined. His proud lance dragged on the carpet.

"Be of good heart," Roddy comforted him. "You are a wonderful imp, and a noble knight, but we will not fight the Rattus norvegicus. We are too small and too few. We will acquiesce and accept their demands."

"You are being my dearest and onliest friend," the Imp complained, "and already you must be leaving."

"I will return anon and again when the requirements and claims of the Brown Rats have been met. During the interlude and interval you must build me a nest in your cave. I am accustomed to dwell high, and such a nest, I know, will satisfy."

The Imp was somewhat gladdened. "I will be getting feathers from Seppy's pillow to be making you a nest. If I am being big enough, and if my cave is being the right size, I am taking Seppy's whole pillow to be making your nest."

"Thank you." Roddy bowed. "Now hop onto my back, and we will be off. The time is short and brief for so much practice. Maybe while I am gone, you can make a saddle and stirrups. When I return you will be ready to ride forth to adventure."

"Already I am thinking about that saddle," exclaimed the Imp. "With my sword I am cutting up one of Seppy's shoes for the leather. I am studding it with diamonds and pearls from the mother's jewelry box. It is being the most princely saddle in the world, sparkling, with silky trappings."

Roddy shuddered at the word trappings. The Imp slapped his forehead. "I am being a stupid imp without any diploma. I am not meaning to remind you of traps."

"I have no right or reason for being so thin-skinned and hypersensitive. Come, we will ride and make memories to remember while we are apart."

The Imp placed the beaded end of the lance in the socket of his hip. Roddy cantered around the living room and under the chairs. As he loped along he sang:

> I am not an ordinary mouse.
> I don't live in anybody's house.
> Cheese and crackers,
> Midnight snackers
> Hold no appeal for me;
> For, you see,
> I am not an ordinary mouse.

"Bravo! Bravo!" cried the Imp. And Roddy continued:

> I am not an ordinary mouse.
> I am host to neither flea nor louse.
> Fear that freezes,
> And diseases
> Are not spread by me;
> For, you see,
> A high treetop is where I make my house!

The Imp, trying to clap and hold the lance in place at the same time, almost fell from Roddy's back. He grabbed hold just in time, for Roddy swerved and headed down the hall.

Drip was doing what cats do instead of sleeping. With his eyes closed, he lay under the kitchen cabinet, letting laziness soak more fully into his soul. A cat, after all, is only three letters inside an envelope of laziness.

Drip didn't love anybody or anything. It was sufficient, he thought, to allow himself to be loved. He harbored one hate, however; the one hate his laziness would allow. He hated mice with a red fervor bred into him through ages of antecedents.

Drip heard the sound, like the tattoo of fingernails on the arm of a chair, as Roddy came galloping down the hall. A force, a current conducted down the centuries by his forebears, hackled the hairs on his back, while, with one fluid movement, he gained his feet. His forefeet were close to his hind, his body in a bristly arc. He looked like a sample left by the Fuller Brush man.

Through the alcove and into the kitchen Roddy bore the Imp. Had Roddy been an ordinary mouse, he would never have raced so toward disaster. He might have smelled a cat. In the center of the kitchen he slid to a standstill. The lance danced in his hand as the Imp looked, with fear and trembling, into Drip's candle-lit eyes. Drip spat and fumed, and trembled no little himself. Had Roddy alone confronted him, he would have disposed of the mouse with the utmost dispatch. But a mouse bearing an imp, and an imp bearing a lance were a befuddling spectacle. Hissing and spitting, he backed under the kitchen cabinet. In Drip's fear the Imp found courage. He dug his knees into Roddy's side.

"Charging!" he cried.

Roddy leaped forward, and the Imp aimed the lance at Drip's eye. The cat flashed his paw in front of his face to ward off the thrust. The point of the lance nicked the flesh pad under his claw. He spat venomously. Complaining like violin strings under a crude bow, he retreated further. The Imp took his mount back ten paces, set his lance once more, and, leaning forward, cried again: "Be charging!"

Roddy, his spirit up to the game, catapulted forward. But Drip was back to the wall, and the wall gave him volition. With his head buried in his shoulders, spitting like a boiling kettle, he met the charge. His paw snapped out. Roddy caught the blow on the side of the head and shot precipitately down a gulf of blackness. The Imp was hurled from under the cabinet, and, with lance still clutched in hand, rolled across the floor.

Disassociated from a rider, Roddy was only a mouse. Drip struck him with both paws a fury of blows. Roddy was broken and limp. Drip nudged him and cautiously nosed his fur.

Unhurt, the Imp climbed to his feet. His impulse was to flee to the safety of his cave. He knew he had lost Roddy, his only friend. He had felt the fatal tearing power of the cat's paw. He wanted to run and cry. Unmounted, he felt impotent and puny. He and Roddy had been having their first game, and had charged Drip not through animosity but enthusiasm. His sorrow over the loss of his friend was too full, for the moment, to permit anger at Drip who was still softly boxing the mouse with his paw. In the eyes of the Imp, Drip was monstrous. However, grasping his lance firmly, he approached the cat.

"Be stopping what you are doing!"

Drip was emboldened by conquest. As the Imp stepped toward him, he crouched, his face almost between his paws.

"You are, no doubting, the biggest drip in the world!"

Drip gauged the distance between him and the Imp.

"You are killing a wonderful mouse. He is having a beautiful voice."

Drip sprang. The Imp, for a fraction of a fraction, watched the cat descending upon him like a yellow cloud. As he leaped to the side, Drip's claw raked off his cap.

"You are trying to snatch me bald-headed," he shouted as he stabbed at the cat. The point of the lance pricked the flesh. Snarling, Drip bounded sideways. The Imp drove the lance forward with all his might. His aim was high. The lance drove harmlessly through the hair on Drip's back and the Imp, carried by the impetus of his drive, plunged into the cat's side. For the veriest moment his mouth was full of hair, and his face buried in a jungle of fur. He was in dreadful peril; for Drip, athirst for another kill, skewered around to reach him. Abandoning his lance, employing hands, teeth and feet, the Imp pulled himself up, and dug in on Drip's back. In a contortion, Drip bit at him. The Imp, as usual, had forgotten to take in his tail. Drip sank his teeth into it.

"Be letting go. Oh-o-o-o-o-o, be letting go that tail!"

Drip tugged at the tail. The Imp was frenzied. "It is being pulled out by the roots. Please be unbiting it," he pleaded.

Drip yanked harder.

Desperately, the Imp pushed his face down through the fur and bit into the cat's back.

Drip released the tail and simultaneously shot two feet straight up from the floor. He landed on all four feet and took off like a sneeze. He sped the length of the kitchen and leaped to the seat of a chair. From the chair he sprang to the table. The Imp clung to the fur and continued to hold with his teeth. On the table, Drip tried again to reach the tormenting thing on his back. He curled like a whirlpool. The Imp sank his teeth deeper and tasted blood. From the table Drip leaped to the shelf above the refrigerator. The small boxes of cereal flew out like stones from a dynamited mountainside. The leap almost dislodged the Imp. He lost hold with his hands, and, for a breathless infinitude, held on only with his teeth. He clawed for a fresh grip, and jabbed his thumb into Drip's left eye. Screeching, Drip shot out into space. As he leaped, the Imp's tail flew up. The barb hooked through a link of the chain suspending the light. The Imp was jerked from the cat's back.

Drip, sailing on across the narrow kitchen, plunged through the glass of the kitchen cabinet door. Shattered, the glass rained down upon the floor. Drip landed on the second shelf, dislodging cups and saucers. The saucers smashed on the ledge of the cabinet. The cups clanked, rolled and bounced to break on the floor. The sugar bowl fell to the ledge, cracked and vomited sugar. Terrified by the din of destruction, Drip tried to crawl into the corner behind the cookie jar. He only succeeded in shoving it from the shelf. It clumped on the ledge, bumped on the floor, and rolled the length of the kitchen.

When the Imp was dragged from Drip's back, he crossed his arms over his head, expecting to plummet down to the floor. However, while the seeming thunder of the falling dishes reverberated in the small kitchen, he swung back and forth unharmed.

"Goodness and gracious," he moaned, "this is being enough to waken my enemies from the dead."

Quickened by that thought and assisted by the fullness of his swinging, he twisted and caught hold of his tail. Through the noise of the limp-like gait of the cookie jar careening across the floor, he heard the father thumping, with feet only halfway into his shoes, out of the bedroom. He clambered up his tail, grasped the chain and released his barb. He looked wildly about him. The floor was too far for a jump. The shelf over the refrigerator too far to reach. The kitchen cabinet, even could he have reached it, was out of the question because there cowed Drip. Only one direction was open. The Imp went up. Link by link he ascended until he reached the ceiling. Putting one leg through the top link, he clung for dear life. He expected the worst—if there could be a worst beyond the loss of his friend, Roddy.

CHAPTER 19

Feeling his way in the dark, kicking fragments of cups and saucers, the father punched at the light button on the wall. He held a "Big Ben" clock in one hand, a weapon in case of attack. He was nervous. Jabbing repeatedly with his thumb, he failed to make contact with the button.

"It's been moved," he muttered. "This whole house has gone wacky."

Panic began to possess him, and he poked frantically. If he failed to get the light on, he felt sure that a disaster of immense proportions would befall him. He began slapping the wall with his open hand.

"Where is the confounded thing?" His thoughts quavered. "Button, button, who took the danged button? Lord, I'm getting hysterical."

He ventured a step forward, and chills, like small cold feet, ran down his spine; for he looked squarely into two demonical eyes. They were on a level with his own. He tried to ask: Who are you? His voice had gone on vacation. He tried again, and emitted only a blubbering sound. My goodness, he thought, I've become a drooling idiot. With heroic courage he overcame a semi-paralysis; and with all his strength hurled the clock at the burning eyes.

The clock missed Drip. It struck the wooden panel of the lower door of the kitchen cabinet. The panel cracked with the noise of thunder, while the whole cabinet shook as under an earthquake. Plates, bowls, platters landed all at once on the floor, crashing, shattering, splintering, ringing. Drip forsook his swaying perch, and hid under the cabinet.

In her bed above the kitchen, Septuagesima lay, covered up to the neck, clutching the blankets, praying: "O Lord, deliver thy servant from this house of maniacs."

"What's the matter? What's happened?" The mother clattered into the kitchen. Alice and Allen were running down the hall.

"Keep back!" The father ordered. "I knocked him out with the clock. He's on the floor. Stay in the hall. He might have a gun."

"Hurry," urged mother. "I'll keep the children in the hall."

The father found the light switch. He had to close his eyes against the sudden brilliance. He squinted after a second. His eyes flew open. The kitchen was a shambles, but no burglar lay amidst the destruction.

"He escaped," the father whispered hoarsely. "He must have gotten past me."

"What shall we do?" asked the mother. "You think he's somewhere in the house? Are you sure there was a burglar?" she pressed the children close to her.

"Of course, I'm sure. Wait here 'til I get my hammer."

"What are you going to do with the hammer?" Alice was curious and unafraid.

"Sh-h-h-h-h," hissed Alan. "He's going to kill the burglar."

"I don't want my daddy to kill a burglar," Alice wailed.

"Be still, Alice. Be still," the father urged.

"Everybody wants me to be still, 'specially when you want to kill a burglar."

"Good heavens," the father moaned. "Can't you keep her quiet?" he begged the mother.

The mother patted Alice, and they followed the father to the tool chest. The mother suddenly remembered Septuagesima.

"Seppy isn't here. Maybe the burglar came in through her window. Maybe he did something to her."

"He couldn't pick a more deserving person," the father mumbled. "I'll search her room first."

"We'll all search" the mother asserted.

"How can I sneak up on him with all of you tramping behind me!"

"We're coming. He'll run away when he sees he's outnumbered."

They ascended the steps to find Septuagesima's door locked. Rapping, the father called out: "Seppy, are you all right?"

"What do you want?" Seppy's voice was harsh.

"Are you all right? Open the door."

"Yes, I'm all right; and I intend to stay all right."

"Open the door, will you. There's a burglar in the house. We want to search your room."

"Over my dead body," was Seppy's reply.

"Maybe he's holding a gun to her ribs and making her say that," the mother suggested.

"That would tickle something awful," Alice giggled.

Alan shushed her. "You want to go back to bed and miss Daddy hitting the burglar with the hammer?"

The father raised the hammer as though he would break in Seppy's door. The mother restrained him. "You'll only frighten her out of her wits."

"She's the most uncooperative character I've ever known." The father grunted with disgust. "I don't think a burglar would stay in the same room with her."

The mother called to the immured cook. "Come now, Seppy, there's nothing to be afraid of."

"First you tell me there's a burglar in the house. Then you say there's nothing to be afraid of. I heard what went on downstairs. When I come out, I'll have my bags packed. I'm quitting. I'm leaving this terrible house."

"Why don't you pack up and go now?" the father growled.

"You'd put me out in the dead of night, in the freezing cold," Seppy screeched. "You're a monster."

"Leave her alone," the mother urged, "she's overwrought."

"I'd like to tap her on her bony head with this hammer," grumbled the father. "We're trying to catch the burglar, and she locks herself up like a chaste maid in a tower."

"It isn't Seppy who's chased; it's the burglar," said Alice.

"He's probably gotten away by now," said the father. "Come, we'll search downstairs anyway."

They hastened down the steps, while the Imp, hearing them descending, clung tighter to the light chain and pushed closer to the ceiling.

Alice brought the caravan to a halt in the kitchen.

"Look at the poor little mouse!" She rushed to Roddy half buried in the shards of kitchenware. Drip moved piteously.

The father felt a premonition that a dreadful discovery was about to be made. The mother looked at him. In her eyes was a mixture of sternness, disappointment, amazement and a tinge of inner mirth.

"Is it possible?" she asked wonderingly.

He sought some semblance of defense. "Is what possible? Alice, let the mouse alone."

"Did you see this burglar?" the mother asked.

"I saw his eyes."

"Wasn't it dark?"

"I tell you, I saw eyes."

"Whose eyes?"

"I saw two eyes that were level with mine," the father got his teeth into the meat of a reasonable defense. "I wasn't standing in a hole, which is about the only evidence of war this kitchen floor lacks, and I wasn't on my hands and knees. So, if the eyes were level with mine, it couldn't have been Drip."

The mother went, "Minini, minee, minee."

Drip put out a cautious head from under the kitchen cabinet. He studied the field of rubble, and was about to retreat again. The mother called. Drip came out hesitantly, one slow step at a time. When he rubbed himself against the mother's leg, he meowed plaintively. He had been in battle.

"No, no, it can't be," the father muttered. "I must be losing my alleged mind. Alice, let that mouse alone!"

"It's got a bandage on its tail. Do they have nurse mouses to bandage injured mouses' tails?" Alice asked.

"And look," cried Alan, "there's the cap off your doll. But where's the rest of the clothes?"

The Imp trembled on his perch. He felt that a dragnet was closing about him.

The father fanned his fingers across his eyes. "Good heavens, what next?"

"There must be some explanation," the mother stated.

"And if she's finding the explanation," the Imp fought against his pounding heart, "I am being a dead ducking."

"Sure, there's an explanation," the father proffered. "It's that grisly, grim, ungainly, gaunt and ghastly cook. She was down here in the kitchen, up to some devilment, and I caught her at it. I threw the clock at her, and that's why she locked herself in. She probably has a new knob on her head."

The Imp had had a hectic night. Hanging to the chain was rapidly exhausting him. However, hearing Septuagesima accused lightened his heavy heart and renewed his strength. "I'm hoping she is hanging in the morning." He looked upon the father with approval. Still, he dared hardly breathe lest one of the group look ceiling-ward and detect him.

The mother told the father that he was childish, that it was evident that the clock had hit nothing but the cabinet door. He told her that nothing but the grace of God saved him from premature senility. The mother reserved her retort for a more private conversation, tightened the girdle of her kimono and hustled the children bed-ward.

"Come, Alan. Come, Alice." She prodded them. "When it's daylight this will look less a mess, and will be easier to clean up."

"Can I please take the mouse to bed with me?" Alice pleaded.

"Definitely not."

"You think I always wanta sleep by myself. I never take anything to bed, no candy or sandwiches either." Alice was indignant.

"You'll get a chill in this cold kitchen," the mother told her. "Dead mice need to be buried. Children don't take them to bed. They have fleas."

The Imp's eyes filled with tears to hear Roddy accused of having fleas. "I'll be doing her something one of these days. I am taking every one of her gems to be decorating my saddle." He remembered then that there would be no use for a saddle. His splendid mount was dead. A spasm of grief almost toppled him from his link.

"Please come to bed," the mother urged the father. "We'll clean up after we've had more sleep." She took Alice and Alan by their hand. At the kitchen doorway she paused. "I don't suppose it would be worthwhile to take the clock."

The father had nothing to reply.

CHAPTER 20

The father seldom had difficulty going to sleep. Ordinarily, he had only to close his eyes to be dead to the world. There were times when he had hardly time to lie down before sleep overtook him. He had never need to seek Morpheus. Morpheus sought him. Following his assault upon Drip, however, the father lay awake. The mysteries of the past nights plagued him. He knew Seppy had not been in the kitchen. Seppy would not have come within a voluntary mile of a mouse, especially a mouse with a first-aided tail.

If it had been Drip who had looked him in the eye like a demon in the dark, what was Drip doing in the kitchen cabinet? How explain the doll clothes, the cookie jar, the missing shoe, the flooded kitchen and the peculiar looking mouse with the bandaged tail? Had a mischievous leprechaun taken up habitation in the house? Possibly, it would all turn out nicely with a pot of gold under the bed.

The father had no liking for lying awake alone; therefore he shook the mother. She sighed and opened her eyes.

"Do you believe in ghosts or leprechauns?" he asked.

The mother was aggrieved. "What'd you say?"

I simply asked if you believe in ghosts or leprechauns."

"Male or female?"

"I didn't know I had wed a wiseacre. Do you realize the situation in this house is becoming increasingly peculiar?"

"You have added to it no little," the mother rejoined. "Throwing the clock through the kitchen cabinet was a peculiar thing for a grown man to do."

"Grant I threw the clock at the cat; but will you kindly inform me, from your womanly wisdom, what Drip was doing in the kitchen cabinet?"

"Was Drip in the kitchen cabinet? Or was your aim so poor?"

The father punched the pillow. "I'll not be made a fool of in my own bed. I've a good mind to hold a coroner's inquest on that mouse with the bandaged tail."

"If you don't let me get some sleep," the mother warned him, "you'll have to fix your own breakfast. Seppy, you remember, has served us notice."

"I'll shed no tears over the loss of Seppy."

"You have no need," said the mother bitingly. "Seppy is my loss."

"I'll fix the breakfast," he proffered.

"Bed time story," the mother derided. "I won't be able to get you out of bed."

"Well, if you decide to serve breakfast in bed, make mine over lightly. Don't break the yellow."

The mother deigned no reply. She grunted and buried her face in the pillow.

"How good it will be," sighed the father, "to eat eggs once more that have not suffered Seppy's mayhem."

When Alice was excited, no part of her escaped the excitement. Her eyebrows moved up to her hairline. She made sucking and gurgling noises as though talking to herself in a unique tongue. Her breath was short, her hands butterflies, and she wiggled her toes. She, like the father, could not sleep. Unlike the father, she had no intention of trying to sleep. Who could go to sleep when there was a mouse on the kitchen floor?

With the child's early-acquired cunning, she waited until sleep had returned to the house. Patting her stomach to make certain that her sleeper was completely buttoned, she slipped from her bed. The light, still burning in the kitchen, cast a slab of illumination into the alcove at the end of the hall. Not forgetting, even in her excitement, the mother's warning not to soil the soles of her sleeper, Alice hastened on barely tip toes to the kitchen.

When his enemies, putting aside the enigmas of the night, had gone again to bed, the Imp had sighed with relief. Then he sighed again over the demise of the gallant Roddy. A third time he sighed with combined relief, sorrow and aloneness. "I guess I'm the sighenist imp in the whole world," he sighed.

Having sighed away some of his depression, the Imp withdrew his leg from the link of the chain. He slapped his calf vigorously. "It is going to sleep while my enemies are hunting burglars. A pin and needle factory is being opened up in my leg."

He descended the chain. "In no time flat I am quitting this house to be carrying the torch for Roddy. I am hating the thought of leaving the princess with the spun golden hair; but duty is calling with loud voices." Reaching the end of the chain, he almost scorched himself on the hot electric bulb. Re-ascending a safe distance, he examined the situation.

"This is being no bowl of cherries," he decided. "I am being up a tree, out on a limb and at the end of my roping."

He looked to where Roddy lay on the floor. He wished with all the fervor of his black heart that Roddy could advise him. Roddy, who had forded rivers, climbed mountains, crossed a continent, could surely have shown him a simple manner of getting down from the light chain.

"But he is sleeping the sleep," mourned the Imp. "And I am having to get into his shoes, being the Spartan, the courier, the drummerdary. But if I am not getting myself off this chain, I am ending up being nothing but a broken-necked imp."

The Imp closed his eyes tight in order to think with the utmost clarity. He thought and thought until the seconds, told by the beating of his heart, began to pound in his ears. The heat rising from the hot globe below him enveloped him with drowsiness. With all his thinking, he could devise no means of freeing himself. He opened his eyes in desperation.

"Goodness and gracious" he ejaculated, "it is being the princess."

Alice had come so quietly on her padded feet that the Imp had been unaware of her presence in the kitchen. With tenderness she was picking up Roddy. She lay the small body on the seat of a chair, and smoothed the soft fur. She hummed, the while, a tuneless tune.

"Maybe she is helping me," thought the Imp. "She is being gentle with Roddy. Maybe she is being gentle with me."

He decided that he had nothing to lose by asking the princess for assistance. He must somehow get down, or, exhausted, ultimately drop off to death on the floor. How could he attract her attention without frightening her? Affrighted, she might give the alarm to all his enemies.

"If I am singing, maybehaps I am charming the princess from being afraid."

The thought was father to action. Hooking his foot in one link and attaching his tail to another for support, he stood up. Holding with one hand, he threw out the other in a gesture of appeal. In an emaciated tenor, he sang:

I am only an Imp on a gilded chain,
A sorrowful sight to see;
If you will giving me freedom again,
How happy you'll making me be.

His voice in the still kitchen was a thin blue ribbon of sound. Alice heard him, and was unafraid. No more would she have been afraid of Snow White or Little Tom Thumb. She looked here and there to locate the singer.

"Princess, princess! I am being up here by the light."

"I can't see you," said Alice. "The light's too bright. I can't even look, the light's so bright."

"Be coming over here and standing under the light."

She stood under the light and looked up, but she had to close her eyes. "The light fills up all my eyes," she complained.

"Just be standing there a minute, and I'm coming down on your shoulder." He hooked his barb in the lowest link, and lowered himself.

"My goodness," Alice exclaimed, "are you Tom Thumb?"

"Please be waiting a second, princess, while I'm unhooking this tail of mine."

He flipped the tail, and the barb came loose. Looping down, the tip of the tail struck Alice on the head.

"Is every bit of that tail yours?" she asked.

"I am being a careless Imp with no carefulness." Standing on tiptoe on her shoulder, and holding on to her ear, he rubbed the spot where the barb had hit. "Every bit is being my own. And ever night it is being burnt and bit, knocked and knotted, scratched and scraped, and entailing untold trouble. When I am being a bigger imp, I am trading it in for a littler one."

"How'd you get such a long tail? Did you catch on something and get stretched like the elephant's trunk?"

The Imp laughed ho, ho, and ha, ha; and almost guffawed himself off Alice's shoulder. Balancing, with a tighter grip on the lobe of Alice's ear, he held up his tail. "I am being born with it just like it is, minus a few scars and a knot."

"Let me hold you in my hand," said Alice. "You might fall off." She cupped her hands, and he sat down as in a cradle.

Filled with joy over meeting the princess and finding her good, the Imp forgot the trials of the past hours, and veritably bulged with glee.

"My goodness," discovered Alice, "you're wearing my doll's clothes; and how'd you ever get them so black!"

"I am not living in a crystal ball or a marble bathtub," the Imp replied. "A cave in the chimney is where I am living; and chimneys, I am having reason to believe, are sometimes dirty."

"But how'd you get up in the chimney?"

"I am being nimble and agile, and, all in alling, a good climber."

"But where've you been? How'd you get in the chimney in the first place? Where's your father and mother? Where'd you come from? My goodness, what's your name? Let me show you to Alan." Alice could not restrain herself as the wonder of the Imp grew.

He stood up in Alice's hands. "O no, princess, do not be showing me to anybody. Everybody, excepting you, is being my enemy, especially that Seppy cook."

"But Alan will love you, and we'll build a most beautiful house for you, all nice and clean."

"Please, don't be doing it," the Imp begged. "I am not being able to stay. Tomorrow I must be going away. I am finding a mission in life."

The father turned in his sleep. The bedspring creaked. The creak, somewhat muffled, traveled to the kitchen.

"My goodness," whispered Alice, "we must get out of the kitchen before daddy wakes up."

The Imp reclined, with legs crossed, on Alice's pillow. She, like a diminutive squaw, squatted in the middle of the bed. She pulled the blanket up around her shoulders. Through the few remaining hours of the night, the Imp recounted his exploits and the near catastrophes that had occupied his nights. Alice smothered her giggles in the blankets when the Imp described his foray into Septuagesima's room. The tears dripped from her wide, sympathetic eyes as the Imp detailed the adventures and sudden death of the eloquent Roddy. When dawn, creeping gray through window, began to give shape to the room, he made Alice solemnly promise that she would tell no one about him. She in turn made him promise that he would visit her that night as soon as the fire in the grate was out. Then he was off to his cave, composing, as he ran, a song about the princess with the spun golden hair. Alice closed her eyes, but, between them and sleep, stood the Impulsive Imp and the wonder of her discovering him.

CHAPTER 21

I t seemed that the earth had fallen out of favor and the sun was not warm to it. The sky was gray; the trees were still, seeming to conserve their strength to bear further burdens of snow and ice.

The mother rose reluctantly to face the day. Once up, however, she hurried from room to room, her housecoat swishing, to light the heaters. She found Alice awake.

"I'm getting out of this darn bed right now," said Alice, taking the bold approach.

"You definitely are not," the mother replied.

"But I must get up."

"You definitely must not."

"But you know yourself, Daddy said I could help him bury Roddy."

"Bury who?"

"I mean the mouse," Alice quickly amended.

"Good heavens, Alice, giving a name to a dead mouse!"

"Well, Mickey Mouse has got a name."

"You may get up as soon as the room gets warm." The mother laid out Alice's clothes.

While the mother cleared the kitchen of the previous night's debacle, the father, escorted by Alice and Alan, carried Roddy's body into the back yard. The children, with mittened hands, scooped the snow from a small space in the hoar-bound garden. The father dug a hole with Alan's Boy Scout hatchet; and Alice was given the honor of setting into the hole the cigar box encasing the defunct Roddy. Tears glistened on Alice's long lashes.

"Aw, it's only a mouse." Alan was being a man about it.

"He must've been a wunnerful, wunnerful mouse." Alice ground at her eyes with wooly fists. She determined that she would write Roddy's name on her slate, and place it as head stone for the grave. The Imp would be glad.

Septuagesima could be heard noisily pushing in drawers, slamming the door of her clothes closet. She was packing to leave. Listening and awaiting her descent, the family ate in silence. The father debated whether or not he should accuse her of being a witch. The mother was deciding that she would maintain her pride and not ask Seppy to stay. On the other hand, supposing the old cook had no place to go. And, with Seppy gone, she would have all the cooking and house work to do herself. Reasonable help simply was not to be had. Suddenly Alice became the focus of attention. The tip of her nose dipped into the milk of her cereal bowl. She was falling to sleep.

"Alice," the father commanded, "eat your cereal. Don't bathe in it."

The mother defended Alice. No wonder the child was sleepy. She had been dragged through the house, searching for burglars in the middle of the night.

"All right," the father granted, "she may leave the table and go back to bed—where she should have stayed last night."

"Please carry me," Alice begged him. "I'm sleepy all over, my legs too."

Septuagesima came down the steps. They creaked under her, and creaked again in surprise. Never before had they occasion to creak under the gaunt Seppy. She seemed ordinarily to carry hardly enough weight to swing a swing. On this doleful morning, however, she lugged her luggage. Her back was bent almost double with the bulging suitcases that rubbed her legs. It seemed that any moment her arms might part from the shoulder. The mother was touched.

Septuagesima stood, knobby and adamantine, saying no word.

"Are you sure you want to leave?" the mother ventured.

"Ma'am, I'll not spend another night in this house."

"But, have you a place to go?"

"I've never been a spendthrift, Ma'am. I'll be able to take care of myself, thank you."

The father wanted to pay her for the full month; but she insisted he pay her only what she had earned. When he pressed her to take more, she snapped: "I'm no beggar; give me my due."

The father thought if she got her due, she'd probably go up in smoke. He held his peace, however, and handed her the money. Gripping her bags, she stomped across the kitchen, through the door and out into the snow. Having said good-bye to no one, neither did she turn her head. She pushed through the gloomy day, appearing much like a scarecrow that had quit its stick and taken on ungainly flight.

"Why don't you get a broom!" the father shouted after her. He was testing his witch theory. Septuagesima did not turn her head; but, having heard, she was convinced the father was a madman. She hurried on her way.

The mother chided the father, saying she was astonished by his cruelty. The father denied being cruel. The mother insisted he was heartless. He offered to let her feel the beating of his heart. She told him it was too bad she had no way of feeling his brain. Exasperated, he stated: "Septuagesima is a witch!"

The mother told him he must have had to go far to fetch an idea like that. He retorted: "In this house, you can fetch any fantastic idea you want without going two steps."

The mother advised him to fetch himself up short when he began to have ideas that cooks are witches.

"You'll see," said the father, "with rags, bones and a hank of hair out of the house, mysterious things will stop happening."

"Maybe worse things will happen," said the mother. "Perhaps Seppy's quitting is only another in a sequence of happenings."

Possibly the mother had a premonition.

"Don't be a pessimist," the father said. "Why should anything worse happen? You can take it from me, that grim cook just didn't like me. Every morning, I think, she tried to poison me."

"Seppy was mortally afraid of you," the mother told him.

"Afraid of me! Why should she be afraid of me? Why, I'm not even permitted to talk loud in this house."

"Nonsense," the mother scoffed, "you throw things around this house. But that's beside the point. Seppy was afraid of you. The salt in her soup, the mouse traps all snapped, and the mouse with the bandaged tail: the children couldn't have done those things."

"Are you implying—? Do you mean—? The father slapped his forehead. "I'm being persecuted." He drew himself up haughtily, and hung out his pride. "I'd prefer to consider your never having said that." He strode from the kitchen, going off to nurse his injured pride.

The mother shook her head worriedly, and went in to check Alice. In her sleep Alice had pushed her stub nose into the pillow. Half her lips smiled. The mother felt a quick, secret, unreasonable fear such as all mothers must feel when they behold their children asleep and utterly helpless.

The gloomy day, with hardly perceptible change, slipped into night. The Imp awoke to an aura of sweet expectancy. Awaiting his coming, no doubting, was the princess. Far below his cave, however, the flames filled up the grate as the father kicked another log higher upon the heap. The father had set himself to solve the riddles of his house; and the solution, besides taking hours, was eating up the logs.

"It has all the looking," grumbled the Imp, "that somebody is trying to decimating the forests."

To help the time pass, he busied himself about his cave. He pushed out the fresh accumulation of soot. With his fingernails he picked at the particles of grit in the porous bricks. He spat upon the bricks, and tried to scrub them clean. The palms of his hands were made dirtier. He rubbed his hands on his trousers; but, since they were more soiled than his hands, he succeeded only in making his palms shine blackly.

"I am knowing nothing so nice as dirt," he decided, "but if the princess is not liking dirt, I will be washing my hands."

He climbed up the chimney. The snow on the bricks at the top had melted from the intensity of the father's fire. The Imp was relieved. "I guess I am being born a dirty Imp, anyway. The princess is maybe liking me dirty like I am." He returned to his cave to watch for the flames in the grate to subside.

The father caught his head just before it struck his chest in a nod. Standing up and stretching for the ceiling, he yawned.

"Might as well go to bed," he told himself. "Can't figure anything out. I might as well buy a crystal ball or go to a misfortune teller."

Having come to know the princess, the Imp was repossessed with all his old impulsiveness. The fire in the grate was dying out much more slowly than his patience. While the flames still laughed high, his patience was exhausted. He climbed down to the ledge and beetled out over the fire. Lying there, he ranted:

Be going out you flames lickety-split.
Be going out, or I'll spit and spit.
Be going out just a little bit,
Or I'll be throwing a conniption fit.

He poked out his tongue, squinted his eyes, and pulled down his brow. The flames leaped up spasmodically as though playfully threatening to reach up for him. He pounded his fists on the bricks.

"O what a contratempting this is being! The princess is waiting for my coming; and I can't be coming out until the fire is going out. Any day now, I am making appeals to the Housing Administration. It is being most unfair to be building conflagrations under my house. My enemies can't be doing this to me."

He marched back and forth on the ledge. Each time he turned he spat vehemently into the flames. The logs, finally, were eaten up. Here and there a jet of flame sprang up, burned brightly for a moment and went out.

"I am waiting no longer," the Imp exclaimed. "The princess, no doubting, is going to sleep betimes."

He wound his tail around his waist and tucked in the barb. Looking down at the embers and gray ashes, he prepared to cast a last powerful invective. Thereupon, he lost his balance and toppled down, his tail unwinding in a graceful arc.

"Yi, yi, yi!" for a moment he was buried in the hot ashes; and then, like a volcano erupting, he sprang up and shot out of the grate. His tail dragged ashes and embers out upon the rug.

"I am roasting and toasting like peanuts," he cried, brushing furiously at the ashes and sparks on his suit. He was unharmed. The doll's clothes had protected him, and his tail and feet were less than scorched. He hastened to the princess, while the red embers ate into the rug.

The slow hours and silence of the house had tricked Alice into sleep.

"Just like I am guessing," murmured the Imp. He sat on the foot of the bed, crossed his legs, folded his arms, and found rapture in just contemplating his idol. "Ah me, I am satisfying to be ugly so her beauty can be telling. Beauty is being in great debt to ugliness."

While he was thinking so profoundly, the evenness of Alice's breathing brought him to nodding. He dreamed that the princess walked through green fields with him sitting upon her shoulder. He could feel the spun golden hair touching and tickling his cheek. He nodded too far and fell out of his dream down into the bed. His weight did not creak the spring or awaken Alice.

"Tonight I am falling all over the place." He sat at Alice's feet. Suddenly his nostrils were assailed, and he noticed that the room was murky with smoke. Alice was stirring restlessly.

"This is being too much smoking. It is looking like my cave when the logs are burning up at me." He slid down the bedpost and ran back to the living room. Flames were running up the walls and licking across the ceiling. He was, for a moment, dumbfounded; and, standing at the threshold, he could only gape at the fire.

"I am spitting myself to death and doing no good here," he thought. "This is being a job for the fire department."

The princess! She was smothering for sure in such billowings of smoke. She was not being a smoke eater like him.

The fire was beginning to be heard. It crackled toward him. He turned and raced to the princess. He put his mouth to Alice's ear and screamed to awaken her. Coughing and rubbing her eyes, Alice sat up in her bed.

"Get up, princess. Be getting up!"

"What's the matter? What's all the smoke?"

"The house is burning down around its ears!"

"Come," urged Alice, "let's go back to mother's room. It'll be safe."

"I can't be going, princess."

"I'll carry you."

"I can't be going. My lance is in my cave, and I am needing it for my journeying."

"You're going now?"

"There is being no better time, I'm thinking."

"But I just found you." The tears eased the smart of the smoke in Alice's eyes. "I don't want you to go."

"But I must be going, sweet princess." The Imp, too, was near to tears, though the smoke hurt his eyes not a bit. "I am having Roddy's commission. I am coming back after I am telling Red's and Roddy's tribes about the Brown Rats."

"But you're so little," said Alice. "You might get hurted."

"I am crossing my heart that I am coming back all right."

"Good-bye, little Imp."

"Good-bye, sweet princess."

While Alice dashed down the hall through the thickening smoke, the Imp faced the flaming living room. "How am I getting through this without being a cooked goose."

The Imp was tempted to flee after Alice, but remembrance of the valiant Roddy lent him courage. Lying flat as he could, he began wriggling his way along the border of the room. The wallpaper curled and crackled above him. Flames and smoke were being sucked with a roar up the chimney. Hugging the bricks, he made his way to the cave.

"I can't be wasting time here," he thought, "or this is being my tomb."

He tucked the lance through the waist of his trousers. Going the remaining length of the chimney, he had to hold on with all his strength. The draft pulled at him; and sparks, like little stars, shot up past him. He reached the top, and a hot gust toppled him over the rim of the chimney down into the soggy snow on the roof. He landed on his back, rolled like a ball down the sloping roof, and fell, with a splash, into the gutter pipe. He had not time to think. Spluttering, he was washed rapidly along. He shot precipitately down a wet blackness. The water shot him out of the spout, throwing him into the yard at the side of the house. He picked himself up, a soaked, shivering, bedraggled imp. The wailing of sirens and the clanging of bells beat upon his ears. Under their greater noise came the constant crunching of snow, and the murmur of the gathering crowd.

The snow easily sustained the Imp. He ran as fast as he could, but his water soaked trousers were a drag on his legs. A fireman's great rubber-booted foot just missed crushing him.

"I am learning too much in nighttime," he complained as he sought the path amongst the feet of those who had run out to see the blazing house.

"Did everybody get out safe?" He heard a man ask, and the Imp paused to hear the reply.

"Yeah, they all got out. But they are having a bad time with the little girl. She was crying like blazes about a little gremlin or something burning up in the house."

"Kids are funny," said the first man, and he laughed.

"Tired warrior though I'm being," growled the Imp, "I am not letting a big lout be laughing at the princess." He yanked the lance from his trousers and jabbed the man's ankle.

"Ouch!" the lout exclaimed, "something bit me."

The Imp hastened away, leaving his victim to nurse his ankle between cold hands.

When his clothes were beginning to stiffen with the cold, the Imp found a haven for the night. It was a little house with an arched doorway.

"It is too bad it is having no door to shut out the wind," the Imp mused, "but it is being a nice size. It is smelling strong like hair; but it is being a friendly smell, almost like Roddy."

He pulled off his wet clothes, and rolled himself up in the piece of red blanket that was pushed into the corner of the little house.

"Whoever is living here, I am telling by the smelling, is not being an enemy. Maybehaps, he is not minding me spending one night. When the sun is up and coming, I am knowing which way is west, and it's westing I am going."

With Roddy close in his memory, and the princess's warm good-bye still music in his ears, the Impulsive Imp went cozily to sleep, while the dog whose house he occupied chased a fire engine down the nearby street.

Made in the USA
Lexington, KY
20 May 2010